D1566202

Selected Short Works by Washington Irving

***Also by Washington Irving
in Large Print:***

The Legend of Sleepy Hollow and Other
   Stories
Rip Van Winkle and Other Stories
Adventures of Captain Bonneville

Selected Short Works by
Washington Irving

Washington Irving

Thorndike Press • Waterville, Maine

Recommended for Middle Readers.

Originally published in 1820 and is now in Public Domain in the United States.

Thorndike Press® Large Print Classics.

The tree indicium is a trademark of Thorndike Press.

The text of this Large Print edition is unabridged.
Other aspects of the book may vary from the original edition.

Set in 16 pt. Plantin by Christina S. Huff.

Printed in the United States on permanent paper.

Library of Congress Cataloging-in-Publication Data

Irving, Washington, 1783–1859.
 [Short stories. Selections]
 Selected short works by Washington Irving.
  p. cm. — (Thorndike Press large print classics)
 ISBN 0-7862-8539-7 (lg. print : hc : alk. paper)
 1. Large type books. I. Title. II. Series.
PS2052 2006
 813′.2—dc22   2006001524

To my daughter Susy
and to her daughter
Annie Donnelly
with admiration and love

The Spectre Bridegroom

*A Traveller's Tale**

Shall I not take mine ease in mine inn!
Falstaff.

During a journey that I once made through the Netherlands, I had arrived one evening at the *Pomme d' Or,* the principal inn of a small Flemish village. It was after the hour of the *table d' hôte,* so that I was obliged to make a solitary supper from the relics of its

*The erudite reader, well versed in good-for-nothing lore, will perceive that the above Tale must have been suggested to the old Swiss by a little French anecdote, a circumstance said to have taken place at Paris.

This tale consists of two chapters of *The Sketch Book*, the first an introductory one titled "The Inn Kitchen." — C.N.

ampler board. The weather was chilly; I was seated alone in one end of a great gloomy dining-room, and, my repast being over, I had the prospect before me of a long dull evening, without any visible means of enlivening it. I summoned mine host, and requested something to read; he brought me the whole literary stock of his household, a Dutch family Bible, an almanac in the same language, and a number of old Paris newspapers. As I sat dozing over one of the latter, reading old and stale criticisms, my ear was now and then struck with bursts of laughter which seemed to proceed from the kitchen. Every one that has travelled on the continent must know how favorite a resort the kitchen of a country inn is to the middle and inferior order of travellers; particularly in that equivocal kind of weather, when a fire becomes agreeable toward evening. I threw aside the newspaper, and explored my way to the kitchen, to take a peep at the group that appeared to be so merry. It was composed partly of travellers who had arrived some hours before in a diligence, and partly of the usual attendants and hangers-on of inns. They were seated round a great burnished stove, that might have been mistaken for an altar, at which they were worshipping. It was covered with various kitchen vessels of resplendent brightness; among which steamed and hissed a huge copper tea-kettle. A large lamp threw a strong mass of light upon the group, bringing out many odd features in strong relief. Its yellow rays partially illumined the spacious kitchen, dying duskily away into remote corners, except where they settled, in mellow radiance on the broad side of a flitch of bacon, or were reflected back from well-scoured utensils, that gleamed from the midst of obscurity. A strapping Flemish lass, with long golden pendants in her ears, and a necklace with a golden heart suspended to it, was the presiding priestess of the temple.

Many of the company were furnished with pipes, and most of them with some kind of evening potation. I found their mirth was occasioned by anecdotes, which a little swarthy Frenchman, with a dry weazen face and large whiskers, was giving of his love adventures; at the end of each of which there was one of those bursts of honest unceremonious laughter, in which a man indulges in that temple of true liberty, an inn.

As I had no better mode of getting through a tedious blustering evening, I took my seat near the stove, and listened to a variety of traveller's tales, some very extravagant, and most very dull. All of them, however, have faded from my treacherous memory except one, which I will endeavor to relate. I fear, however, it derived its chief zest from the manner in which it was told, and the peculiar air and appearance of the narrator. He was a corpulent old Swiss, who had the look of a veteran traveller. He was dressed in a tarnished green travelling-jacket, with a broad belt round his waist, and a pair of overalls, with buttons from the hips to the ankles. He was of a full, rubicund countenance, with a double chin, aquiline nose and a pleasant, twinkling eye. His hair was light, and curled from under an old green velvet travelling-cap stuck on one side of his head. He was interrupted more than once by the arrival of guests, or the remarks of his auditors; and paused now and then to replenish his pipe; at which times he had generally a roguish leer, and a sly joke for the buxom kitchen-maid.

I wish my readers could imagine the old fellow lolling in a huge armchair, one arm akimbo, the other holding a curiously twisted tobacco-pipe, formed of genuine *écume de mer,* decorated with silver chain and silken tassel, — his head cocked on one side, and a whimsical cut of the eye occasionally, as he related the following story.

He that supper for is dight,
He lyes full cold, I trow, this night!
Yestreen to chamber I him led,
This night Gray-Steel has made his bed.
Sir Eger, Sir Grahame,
and Sir Gray-Steel.

On the summit of one of the heights of the Odenwald, a wild and romantic tract of Upper Germany, that lies not far from the confluence of the Main and the Rhine, there stood, many, many years since, the Castle of the Baron Von Landshort. It is now quite fallen to decay, and almost buried among beechtrees and dark firs; above which, however, its old watch-tower may still be seen struggling, like the former possessor I have mentioned, to carry a high head, and look down upon the neighboring country.

The baron was a dry branch of the great family of Katzenellenbogen,* and inherited the relics of the property, and all the pride of his ancestors. Though the warlike disposition of his predecessors had much impaired

*I.e., Cat's-Elbow. The name of a family of those parts, very powerful in former times. The appellation, we are told, was given in compliment to a peerless dame of the family, celebrated for her fine arm.

the family possessions, yet the baron still endeavored to keep up some show of former state. The times were peaceable, and the German nobles, in general, had abandoned their inconvenient old castles, perched like eagles' nests among the mountains, and had built more convenient residences in the valleys: still the baron remained proudly drawn up in his little fortress, cherishing, with hereditary inveteracy, all the old family feuds; so that he was on ill terms with some of his nearest neighbors, on account of disputes that had happened between their great-great-grandfathers.

The baron had but one child, a daughter; but nature, when she grants but one child, always compensates by making it a prodigy; and so it was with the daughter of the baron. All the nurses, gossips, and country-cousins assured her father that she had not her equal for beauty in all Germany; and who should know better than they? She had, moreover, been brought up with great care under the superintendence of two maiden aunts, who had spent some years of their early life at one of the little German courts, and were skilled in all the branches of knowledge necessary to the education of a fine lady. Under their instructions she became a miracle of accomplishments. By the time she was eighteen, she could embroider to admiration, and had worked whole histories of the saints in tapestry, with such strength of expression in their countenance, that they looked like so many souls in purgatory. She could read without great difficulty, and had spelled her way through several church legends, and almost all the chivalric wonders of the Heldenbuch. She had even made considerable proficiency in writing; could sign her own name without missing a letter, and so legibly that her aunts could read it without spectacles. She excelled in making little elegant good-for-nothing lady-like knick-knacks of all kinds; was versed in the most abstruse dancing of the day; played a number of airs on the harp and guitar; and knew all the tender ballads of the Minnelieders by heart.

Her aunts, too, having been great flirts and coquettes in their younger days, were admirably calculated to be vigilant guardians and strict censors of the conduct of their niece; for there is no duenna so rigidly prudent, and inexorably decorous, as a superannuated coquette. She was rarely suffered out of their sight; never went beyond the domains of the castle, unless well attended, or rather well watched; had continual lectures read to her about strict decorum and implicit obedience; and as to the men — pah! — she was taught to hold them at such a distance, and in such absolute distrust, that, unless properly authorized, she would not have cast a glance upon the handsomest cavalier in the world — no, not if he were even dying at her feet.

The good effects of this system were wonderfully apparent. The young lady was a pattern of docility and correctness. While others were wasting their sweetness in the glare of the world, and liable to be plucked and thrown aside by every hand, she was coyly blooming into fresh and lovely womanhood under the protection of those immaculate spinsters like a rose-bud blushing forth among guardian thorns. Her aunts looked upon her with pride and exultation, and vaunted that though all the other young ladies in the world might go astray, yet, thank Heaven, nothing of the kind could happen to the heiress of Katzenellenbogen.

But, however scantily the Baron Von Landshort might be provided with children, his household was by no means a small one; for Providence had enriched him with abundance of poor relations. They, one and all, possessed the affectionate disposition common to humble relatives; were wonderfully attached to the baron, and took every possible occasion to come in swarms and enliven the castle. All family festivals were commemorated by these good people at the baron's expense; and when they were filled with good cheer, they would declare that there was nothing on earth so delightful as these family meetings, these jubilees of the heart.

The baron, though a small man, had a large soul, and it swelled with satisfaction at the consciousness of being the greatest man in the little world about him. He loved to tell long stories about the dark old warriors whose portraits looked grimly down from the walls around, and he found no listeners equal to those who fed at his expense. He was much given to the marvellous, and a firm believer in all those supernatural tales with which every mountain and valley in Germany abounds. The faith of his guests exceeded even his own; they listened to every tale of wonder with open eyes and mouth, and never failed to be astonished, even though repeated for the hundredth time. Thus lived the Baron Von Landshort, the oracle of his table, the absolute monarch of his little territory, and happy, above all things, in the persuasion that he was the wisest man of the age.

At the time of which my story treats, there was a great family-gathering at the castle, on an affair of the utmost importance: it was to receive the destined bridegroom of the baron's daughter. A negotiation had been carried on between the father and an old nobleman of Bavaria, to unite the dignity of their houses by the marriage of their children. The preliminaries had been conducted with proper punctilio. The young people were betrothed without seeing each other; and the time was appointed for the marriage ceremony. The young Count Von Altenburg had been recalled from the army for the purpose, and was actually on his way to the baron's to receive his bride. Missives had even been received from him, from Würtzburg, where he was accidentally detained, mentioning the day and hour when he might be expected to arrive.

The castle was in a tumult of preparation to give him a suitable welcome. The fair bride had been decked out with uncommon care. The two aunts had superintended her toilet, and quarrelled the whole morning about every article of her dress. The young lady had taken advantage of their contest to follow the bent of her own taste; and fortunately it was a good one. She looked as lovely as youthful bridegroom could desire;

and the flutter of expectation heightened the lustre of her charms.

The suffusions that mantled her face and neck, the gentle heaving of the bosom, the eye now and then lost in reverie, all betrayed the soft tumult that was going on in her little heart. The aunts were continually hovering around her; for maiden aunts are apt to take great interest in affairs of this nature. They were giving her a world of staid counsel how to deport herself, what to say, and in what manner to receive the expected lover.

The baron was no less busied in preparations. He had, in truth, nothing exactly to do; but he was naturally a fuming, bustling little man, and could not remain passive when all the world was in a hurry. He worried from top to bottom of the castle with an air of infinite anxiety; he continually called the servants from their work to exhort them to be diligent; and buzzed about every hall and chamber, as idly restless and importunate as a blue-bottle fly on a warm summer's day.

In the meantime the fatted calf had been killed; the forests had rung with the clamor of the huntsmen; the kitchen was crowded with good cheer; the cellars had yielded up whole oceans of *Rhein-wein* and *Ferne-wein;* and even the great Heidelberg tun had been laid under contribution. Everything was ready to receive the distinguished guest with *Saus* and *Braus* in the true spirit of German hospitality; — but the guest delayed to make his appearance. Hour rolled after hour. The sun, that had poured his downward rays upon the rich forest of the Odenwald, now just gleamed along the summits of the mountains. The baron mounted the highest tower, and strained his eyes in the hope of catching a distant sight of the count and his attendants. Once he thought he beheld them; the sound of horns came floating from the valley, prolonged by the mountain echoes. A number of horsemen were seen far below, slowly advancing along the road; but when they had nearly reached the foot of the mountain, they suddenly struck off in a different direction. The last ray of sunshine departed, — the bats began to flit by in the twilight, — the road grew dimmer and dimmer to the view, and nothing appeared stirring in it but now and then a peasant lagging homeward from his labor.

While the old castle of Landshort was in this state of perplexity, a very interesting scene was transacting in a different part of the Odenwald.

The young Count Von Altenburg was

tranquilly pursuing his route in that sober jogtrot way, in which a man travels toward matrimony when his friends have taken all the trouble and uncertainty of courtship off his hands, and a bride is waiting for him, as certainly as a dinner at the end of his journey. He had encountered at Würtzburg a youthful companion in arms, with whom he had seen some service on the frontiers, — Herman Von Starkenfaust, one of the stoutest hands and worthiest hearts of German chivalry, who was now returning from the army. His father's castle was not far distant from the old fortress of Landshort, although an hereditary feud rendered the families hostile, and strangers to each other.

In the warm-hearted moment of recognition, the young friends related all their past adventures and fortunes, and the count gave the whole history of his intended nuptials with a young lady whom he had never seen, but of whose charms he had received the most enrapturing descriptions.

As the route of the friends lay in the same direction, they agreed to perform the rest of their journey together; and, that they might do it the more leisurely, set off from Würtzburg at an early hour, the count having given directions for his retinue to follow and overtake him.

They beguiled their wayfaring with recollections of their military scenes and adventures; but the count was apt to be a little tedious, now and then, about the reputed charms of his bride, and the felicity that awaited him.

In this way they had entered among the mountains of the Odenwald, and were traversing one of its most lonely and thickly-wooded passes. It is well known that the forests of Germany have always been as much infested by robbers, as its castles by spectres; and, at this time, the former were particularly numerous, from the hordes of disbanded soldiers wandering about the country. It will not appear extraordinary, therefore, that the cavaliers were attacked by a gang of these stragglers, in the midst of the forest. They defended themselves with bravery, but were nearly overpowered, when the count's retinue arrived to their assistance. At sight of them the robbers fled, but not until the count had received a mortal wound. He was slowly and carefully conveyed back to the city of Würtzburg, and a friar summoned from a neighboring convent, who was famous for his skill in administering to both soul and body; but half of his skill was superfluous; the moments of the unfortunate count were numbered.

With his dying breath he entreated his friend to repair instantly to the castle of Landshort, and explain the fatal cause of his not keeping his appointment with his bride. Though not the most ardent of lovers, he was one of the most punctilious of men, and appeared earnestly solicitous that his mission should be speedily and courteously executed. "Unless this is done," said he, "I shall not sleep quietly in my grave!" He repeated these last words with peculiar solemnity. A request, at a moment so impressive, admitted no hesitation. Starkenfaust endeavored to soothe him to calmness; promised faithfully to execute his wish, and gave him his hand in solemn pledge. The dying man pressed it in acknowledgment, but soon lapsed into delirium — raved about his bride — his engagements — his plighted word; ordered his horse, that he might ride to the castle of Landshort; and expired in the fancied act of vaulting into the saddle.

Starkenfaust bestowed a sigh and a soldier's tear on the untimely fate of his comrade; and then pondered on the awkward mission he had undertaken. His heart was heavy, and his head perplexed; for he was to present himself an unbidden guest among hostile people, and to damp their festivity with tidings fatal to their hopes. Still there were certain whisperings of curiosity in his bosom to see this far-famed beauty of Katzenellenbogen, so cautiously shut up from the world; for he was a passionate admirer of the sex, and there was a dash of eccentricity and enterprise in his character that made him fond of all singular adventure.

Previous to his departure he made all due arrangements with the holy fraternity of the convent for the funeral solemnities of his friend, who was to be buried in the cathedral of Würtzburg, near some of his illustrious relatives; and the mourning retinue of the count took charge of his remains.

It is now high time that we should return to the ancient family of Katzenellenbogen, who were impatient for their guest, and still more for their dinner; and to the worthy little baron, whom we left airing himself on the watch-tower.

Night closed in, but still no guest arrived. The baron descended from the tower in despair. The banquet, which had been delayed from hour to hour, could no longer be postponed. The meats were already overdone; the cook in an agony; and the whole household had the look of a garrison that had been reduced by famine. The baron was obliged reluctantly to give orders for the feast without the presence of the guest. All were seated at table, and just on the point of commencing, when the sound of a horn from without the gate gave notice of the approach of a stranger. Another long blast filled the old courts of the castle with its echoes, and was answered by the warder from the walls. The baron hastened to receive his future son-in-law.

The drawbridge had been let down, and the stranger was before the gate. He was a tall, gallant cavalier, mounted on a black steed. His countenance was pale, but he had a beaming, romantic eye, and an air of stately melancholy. The baron was a little mortified that he should have come in this simple, solitary style. His dignity for a moment was ruffled, and he felt disposed to consider it a want of proper respect for the important occasion, and the important family with which he was to be connected. He pacified himself, however, with the conclusion, that it must have been youthful impatience which had induced him thus to spur on sooner than his attendants.

"I am sorry," said the stranger, "to break in upon you thus unseasonably —"

Here the baron interrupted him with a world of compliments and greetings; for, to tell the truth, he prided himself upon his courtesy and eloquence. The stranger attempted, once or twice, to stem the torrent of words, but in vain, so he bowed his head and suffered it to flow on. By the time the baron had come to a pause, they had reached the inner court of the castle; and the stranger was again about to speak, when he was once more interrupted by the appearance of the female part of the family, leading forth the shrinking and blushing bride. He gazed on her for a moment as one entranced; it seemed as if his whole soul beamed forth in the gaze, and rested upon that lovely form. One of the maiden aunts whispered something in her ear; she made an effort to speak; her moist blue eye was timidly raised; gave a shy glance of inquiry on the stranger; and was cast again to the ground. The words died away; but there was a sweet smile playing about her lips, and a soft dimpling of the cheek that showed her glance had not been unsatisfactory. It was impossible for a girl of the fond age of eighteen, highly predisposed for love and matrimony, not to be pleased with so gallant a cavalier.

The late hour at which the guest had arrived left no time for parley. The baron was peremptory, and deferred all particular conversation until the morning, and led the way to the untasted banquet.

It was served up in the great hall of the castle. Around the walls hung the hard-favored portraits of the heroes of the house of Katzenellenbogen, and the trophies which they had gained in the field and in the chase. Hacked corselets, splintered jousting spears, and tattered banners, were mingled with the spoils of sylvan warfare; the jaws of the wolf, and the tusks of the boar, grinned horribly among cross-bows and battle-axes, and a huge pair of antlers branched immediately over the head of the youthful bridegroom.

The cavalier took but little notice of the company or the entertainment. He scarcely tasted the banquet, but seemed absorbed in admiration of his bride. He conversed in a low tone that could not be overheard — for the language of love is never loud; but where is the female ear so dull that it cannot catch the softest whisper of the lover? There was a mingled tenderness and gravity in his manner, that appeared to have a powerful effect upon the young lady. Her color came and went as she listened with deep attention. Now and then she made some blushing reply, and when his eye was turned away, she would steal a sidelong glance at his romantic countenance, and heave a gentle sigh of tender happiness. It was evident that the young couple were completely enamored. The aunts, who were deeply versed in the mysteries of the heart, declared that they had fallen in love with each other at first sight.

The feast went on merrily, or at least noisily, for the guests were all blessed with those keen appetites that attend upon light purses and mountain-air. The baron told his best and longest stories, and never had he told them so well, or with such great effect. If there was anything marvellous, his auditors were lost in astonishment; and if anything facetious, they were sure to laugh exactly in the right place. The baron, it is true, like most great men, was too dignified to utter any joke but a dull one; it was always enforced, however, by a bumper of excellent Hockheimer; and even a dull joke, at one's own table, served up with jolly old wine, is irresistible. Many good things were said by poorer and keener wits, that would not bear repeating, except on similar occasions; many sly speeches whispered in ladies' ears, that almost convulsed them with suppressed laughter; and a song or two roared out by a poor, but merry and broad-faced cousin of the baron, that absolutely made the maiden aunts hold up their fans.

Amidst all this revelry, the stranger guest maintained a most singular and unseasonable gravity. His countenance assumed a deeper caste of dejection as the evening advanced; and, strange as it may appear, even the baron's jokes seemed only to render him the more melancholy. At times he was lost in thought, and at times there was a perturbed and restless wandering of the eye that bespoke a mind but ill at ease. His conversations with the bride became more and more earnest and mysterious. Lowering clouds began to steal over the fair serenity of her brow, and tremors to run through her tender frame.

All this could not escape the notice of the company. Their gayety was chilled by the unaccountable gloom of the bridegroom; their spirits were infected; whispers and glances were interchanged, accompanied by shrugs and dubious shakes of the head. The song and the laugh grew less and less frequent; there were dreary pauses in the conversation, which were at length succeeded by wild tales and supernatural legends. One dismal story produced another still more dismal, and the baron nearly frightened some of the ladies into hysterics with the history of the goblin horseman that carried away the fair Leonora: a dreadful story, which has since been put into excellent verse, and is read and believed by all the world.

The bridegroom listened to this tale with profound attention. He kept his eyes steadily fixed on the baron and, as the story drew to a close, began gradually to rise from his seat, growing taller and taller, until, in the baron's entranced eye, he seemed almost to tower into a giant. The moment the tale was finished, he heaved a deep sigh, and took a solemn farewell of the company. They were all amazement. The baron was perfectly thunderstruck.

"What! going to leave the castle at midnight? why, everything was prepared for his reception; a chamber was ready for him if he wished to retire."

The stranger shook his head mournfully and mysteriously; "I must lay my head in a different chamber to-night!"

There was something in this reply, and the tone in which it was uttered, that made the baron's heart misgive him; but he rallied his forces, and repeated his hospitable entreaties.

The stranger shook his head silently, but positively, at every offer; and, waving his farewell to the company, stalked slowly out of the hall. The maiden aunts were absolutely petrified; the bride hung her head, and a tear stole to her eye.

The baron followed the stranger to the great court of the castle, where the black charger stood pawing the earth, and snorting with impatience. When they had reached the portal, whose deep archway was dimly lighted by a cresset, the stranger paused, and addressed the baron in a hollow tone of voice, which the vaulted roof rendered still more sepulchral.

"Now that we are alone," said he, "I will impart to you the reason of my going. I have a solemn, an indispensable engagement —"

"Why," said the baron, "cannot you send some one in your place?"

"It admits of no substitute — I must attend it in person — I must away to Würtzburg cathedral —"

"Ay," said the baron, plucking up spirit, "but not until to-morrow — to-morrow you shall take your bride there."

"No! no!" replied the stranger, with tenfold solemnity, "my engagement is with no bride — the worms! the worms expect me! I am a dead man — I have been slain by robbers — my body lies at Würtzburg — at midnight I am to be buried — the grave is waiting for me — I must keep my appointment!"

He sprang on his black charger, dashed over the drawbridge, and the clattering of his horse's hoofs was lost in the whistling of the night-blast.

The baron returned to the hall in the utmost consternation, and related what had passed. Two ladies fainted outright, others sickened at the idea of having banqueted with a spectre. It was the opinion of some, that this might be the wild huntsman, famous in German legend. Some talked of mountain sprites, of wood-demons, and of other supernatural beings, with which the good people of Germany have been so grievously harassed since time immemorial. One of the poor relations ventured to suggest that it might be some sportive evasion of the young cavalier, and that the very gloominess of the caprice seemed to accord with so melancholy a personage. This, however, drew on him the indignation of the whole company, and especially of the baron, who looked upon him as little better than an infidel; so that he was fain to abjure his heresy as speedily as possible, and come into the faith of the true believers.

But whatever may have been the doubts entertained, they were completely put to an end by the arrival, next day, of regular missives, confirming the intelligence of the young count's murder, and his interment in Würtzburg cathedral.

The dismay at the castle may well be imagined. The baron shut himself up in his chamber. The guests, who had come to rejoice with him, could not think of abandoning him in his distress. They wandered about the courts, or collected in groups in the hall, shaking their heads and shrugging their shoulders, at the troubles of so good a man; and sat longer than ever at table, and ate and drank more stoutly than ever, by way of keeping up their spirits. But the situation of the widowed bride was the most pitiable. To have lost a husband before she had even embraced him — and such a husband! if the very spectre could be so gracious and noble, what must have been the living man. She filled the house with lamentations.

On the night of the second day of her widowhood, she had retired to her chamber, accompanied by one of her aunts, who insisted on sleeping with her. The aunt, who was one of the best tellers of ghost-stories in all Germany, had just been recounting one of her longest, and had fallen asleep in the very midst of it. The chamber was remote, and overlooked a small garden. The niece lay pensively gazing at the beams of the rising moon, as they trembled on the leaves of an aspen tree before the lattice. The castle-clock had just tolled midnight, when a soft strain of music stole up from the garden. She rose hastily from her bed, and stepped lightly to the window. A tall figure stood among the shadows of the trees. As it raised its head, a beam of moonlight fell upon the countenance. Heaven and, earth! she beheld the Spectre Bridegroom! A loud shriek at that moment burst upon her ear, and her aunt, who had been awakened by the music, and had followed her silently to the window, fell into her arms. When she looked again, the spectre had disappeared.

Of the two females, the aunt now required the most soothing, for she was perfectly beside herself with terror. As to the young lady, there was something, even in the spectre of her lover, that seemed endearing. There was still the semblance of manly beauty; and though the shadow of a man is but little calculated to satisfy the affections of a lovesick girl, yet, where the substance is not to be had, even that is consoling. The aunt declared she would never sleep in that chamber again; the niece, for once, was refractory, and declared as strongly that she would sleep in no other in the castle: the consequence was, that she had to sleep in it alone; but she drew a promise from her aunt not to relate the story of the spectre, lest she should be denied the only melancholy pleasure left her on earth — that of inhabiting the chamber over which the guardian shade of her lover kept its nightly vigils.

How long the good old lady would have observed this promise is uncertain, for she dearly loved to talk of the marvellous, and there is a triumph in being the first to tell a frightful story; it is, however, still quoted in the neighborhood, as a memorable instance of female secrecy, that she kept it to herself for a whole week; when she was suddenly absolved from all further restraint, by intelligence brought to the breakfast-table one morning that the young lady was not to be found. Her room was empty — the bed had not been slept in — the window was open, and the bird had flown!

The astonishment and concern with which the intelligence was received can only be imagined by those who have witnessed the agitation which the mishaps of a great man cause among his friends. Even the poor relations paused for a moment from the indefatigable labors of the trencher; when the aunt, who had at first been struck speechless, wrung her hands, and shrieked out, "The goblin! the goblin! she's carried away by the goblin!"

In a few words she related the fearful scene in the garden, and concluded that the spectre must have carried off his bride. Two of the domestics corroborated the opinion, for they had heard the clattering of a horse's hoofs down the mountain about midnight, and had no doubt that it was the spectre on his black charger, bearing her away to the tomb. All present were struck with the direful probability; for events of the kind are extremely common in Germany, as many well-authenticated histories bear witness.

What a lamentable situation was that of the poor baron! What a heart-rending dilemma for a fond father, and a member of the great family of Katzenellenbogen! His only daughter had either been rapt away to the grave, or he was to have some wood-demon for a son-in-law, and, perchance, a troop of goblin grandchildren. As usual, he was completely bewildered, and all the castle in an uproar. The men were ordered to take horse, and scour every road and path and glen of the Odenwald. The baron himself had just drawn on his jack-boots, girded on his sword, and was about to mount his steed and sally forth on a doubtful quest, when he was brought to a pause by a new apparition. A lady was seen approaching the castle, mounted on a palfrey, attended by a cavalier on horseback. She galloped up to the gate, sprang from her horse, and falling at the baron's feet, embraced his knees. It was his lost daughter, and her companion — the Spectre Bridegroom! The baron was astounded. He looked at his daughter, then at the spectre, and almost doubted the evidence of his senses. The latter, too, was wonderfully improved in his appearance since his visit to the world of spirits. His dress was splendid, and set off a noble figure of manly symmetry. He was no longer pale and melancholy. His fine countenance was flushed with the glow of youth, and joy rioted in his large dark eye.

The mystery was soon cleared up. The cavalier (for, in truth, as you must have known all the while, he was no goblin) announced himself as Sir Herman Von Starkenfaust. He related his adventure with the young count. He told how he had hastened to the castle to deliver the unwelcome tidings, but that the eloquence of the baron had interrupted him in every attempt to tell his tale. How the sight of the bride had completely captivated him, and that to pass a few hours near her, he had tacitly suffered the mistake to continue. How he had been sorely perplexed in what way to make a decent retreat, until the baron's goblin stories had suggested his eccentric exit. How, fearing the feudal hostility of the family, he had repeated his visits by stealth — had haunted the garden beneath the young lady's window — had wooed — had won — had borne away in triumph — and, in a word, had wedded the fair.

Under any other circumstances the baron would have been inflexible, for he was tenacious of paternal authority, and devoutly obstinate in all family feuds; but he loved his daughter; he had lamented her as lost; he rejoiced to find her still alive; and, though her husband was of a hostile house, yet, thank heaven, he was not a goblin. There was something, it must be acknowledged, that did not exactly accord with his notions of strict veracity, in the joke the knight has passed upon him of his being a dead man; but several old friends present, who had served in the wars, assured him that every strategem was excusable in love, and that the cavalier was entitled to especial privilege, having lately served as a trooper.

Matters, therefore, were happily arranged. The baron pardoned the young couple on the spot. The revels at the castle were resumed. The poor relations overwhelmed this new member of the family with loving-kindness; he was so gallant, so generous — and so rich. The aunts, it is true, were somewhat scandalized that their system of strict seclusion and passive obedience should be so badly exemplified, but attributed it all to their negligence in not having the windows grated. One of them was particularly mortified at having her marvellous story marred, and that the only spectre she had ever seen should turn out a counterfeit; but the niece seemed perfectly happy at having found him substantial flesh and blood — and so the story ends.

From *The Sketch Book*

The Legend of Sleepy Hollow

Found Among the Papers of the Late Diedrich Knickerbocker

A pleasing land of drowsy head it was,
Of dreams that wave before the half-shut
 eye,
And of gay castles in the clouds that pass,
For ever flushing round a summer sky.
                        Castle of Indolence.

In the bosom of one of those spacious coves which indent the eastern shore of the Hudson, at that broad expansion of the river denominated by the ancient Dutch navigators the Tappan Zee, and where they always prudently shortened sail, and implored the protection of St. Nicholas when they crossed, there lies a small market-town or rural port, which by some is called Greensburgh, but which is more generally and properly known by the name of Tarry Town. This name was given, we are told, in former days, by the good housewives of the adjacent country, from the inveterate propensity of their husbands to linger about the village tavern on market-days. Be that as it may, I do not vouch for the fact, but merely advert to it for the sake of being precise and authentic. Not far from this village, perhaps about two miles, there is a little valley, or rather lap of land, among high hills, which is one of the quietest places in the whole world. A small brook glides through it, with just murmur enough to lull one to repose; and the occasional whistle of a quail, or tapping of a woodpecker, is almost the only sound that ever breaks in upon the uniform tranquillity.

I recollect that, when a stripling, my first exploit in squirrel-shooting was in a grove of tall walnut-trees that shades one side of the valley. I had wandered into it at noon-time, when all nature is particularly quiet, and was startled by the roar of my own gun, as it broke the Sabbath stillness around, and was prolonged and reverberated by the angry echoes. If ever I should wish for a retreat, whither I might steal from the world and its distractions, and dream quietly away the remnant of a troubled life, I know of none more promising than this little valley.

From the listless repose of the place, and the peculiar character of its inhabitants, who are descendants from the original Dutch settlers, this sequestered glen has long been known by the name of SLEEPY HOLLOW, and its rustic lads are called the Sleepy Hollow Boys throughout all the neighboring country. A drowsy, dreamy influence seems to hang over the land, and to pervade the very atmosphere. Some say that the place was bewitched by a high German doctor, during the early days of the settlement; others, that an old Indian chief, the prophet or wizard of his tribe, held his pow-wows there before the country was discovered by Master Hendrick Hudson. Certain it is, the place still continues under the sway of some bewitching power, that holds a spell over the minds of the good people, causing them to walk in a continual reverie. They are given to all kinds of marvellous beliefs; are subject to trances and visions; and frequently see strange sights, and hear music and voices in the air. The whole neighborhood abounds with local tales, haunted spots, and twilight superstitions; stars shoot and meteors glare oftener across the valley than in any other part of the country, and the nightmare, with her whole ninefold, seems to make it the favorite scene of her gambols.

The dominant spirit, however, that haunts this enchanted region, and seems to be commander-in-chief of all the powers of the air, is the apparition of a figure on horseback without a head. It is said by some to be the ghost of a Hessian trooper, whose head had been carried away by a cannon-ball, in some nameless battle during the Revolutionary War, and who is ever and anon seen by the country folk, hurrying along in the gloom of night, as if on the wings of the wind. His haunts are not confined to the valley, but extend at times to the adjacent roads, and especially to the vicinity of a church at no great distance. Indeed, certain of the most authentic historians of those parts, who have been careful in collecting and collating the floating facts concerning this spectre, allege that the body of the trooper, having been buried in the churchyard, the ghost rides forth to the scene of battle in nightly quest of his head; and that the rushing speed with which he sometimes passes along the Hollow, like a midnight blast, is owing to his being belated, and in a hurry to get back to the churchyard before daybreak.

Such is the general purport of this legendary superstition, which has furnished materials for many a wild story in that region of shadows; and the spectre is known, at all the country firesides, by the name of the Headless Horseman of Sleepy Hollow.

It is remarkable that the visionary propensity I have mentioned is not confined to the native inhabitants of the valley, but is unconsciously imbibed by every one who resides there for a time. However wide awake they may have been before they entered that sleepy region, they are sure, in a little time, to inhale the witching influence of the air, and begin to grow imaginative, to dream dreams, and see apparitions.

I mention this peaceful spot with all possible laud; for it is in such little retired Dutch valleys, found here and there embosomed in the great State of New York, that population, manners, and customs remain fixed; while the great torrent of migration and improvement, which is making such incessant changes in other parts of this restless country, sweeps by them unobserved. They are like those little nooks of still water which border a rapid stream; where we may see the straw and bubble riding quietly at anchor, or slowly revolving in their mimic harbor, undisturbed by the rush of the passing current. Though many years have elapsed since I trod the drowsy shades of Sleepy Hollow, yet I question whether I should not still find the same trees and the same families vegetating in its sheltered bosom.

In this by-place of nature, there abode, in a remote period of American history, that is to say, some thirty years since, a worthy wight of the name of Ichabod Crane; who sojourned, or, as he expressed it, "tarried," in Sleepy Hollow, for the purpose of instructing the children of the vicinity. He was a native of Connecticut, a State which supplies the Union with pioneers for the mind as well as for the forest, and sends forth yearly its legions of frontier woodsmen and country schoolmasters. The cognomen of Crane was not inapplicable to his person. He was tall, but exceedingly lank, with narrow shoulders, long arms and legs, hands that dangled a mile out of his sleeves, feet that might have served for shovels, and his whole frame most loosely hung together. His head was small, and flat at top, with huge ears, large green glassy eyes, and a long snipe nose, so that it looked like a weathercock perched upon his spindle neck, to tell which way the wind blew. To see him striding along the profile of a hill on a windy day, with his clothes bagging and fluttering about him, one might have mistaken him for the genius of famine descending upon the earth, or some scarecrow eloped from a corn-field.

His school-house was a low building of one large room, rudely constructed of logs; the windows partly glazed, and partly patched with leaves of old copy-books. It was most ingeniously secured at vacant hours by a withe twisted in the handle of the door, and stakes set against the window-shutters; so that, though a thief might get in with perfect ease, he would find some embarrassment in getting out: an idea most probably borrowed by the architect, Yost Van Houten, from the mystery of an eel-pot. The school-house stood in a rather lonely but pleasant situation, just at the foot of a woody hill, with a brook running close by, and a formidable birch-tree growing at one end of it. From hence the low murmur of his pupils' voices, conning over their lessons, might be heard on a drowsy summer's day, like the hum of a bee-hive; interrupted now and then by the authoritative voice of the master, in the tone of menace or command; or, peradventure, by the appalling sound of the birch, as he urged some tardy loiterer along the flowery path of knowledge. Truth to say, he was a conscientious man, and ever bore in mind the golden maxim, "Spare the rod and spoil the child." — Ichabod Crane's scholars certainly were not spoiled.

I would not have it imagined, however, that he was one of those cruel potentates of the school, who joy in the smart of their subjects; on the contrary, he administered justice with discrimination rather than severity, taking the burden off the backs of the weak, and laying it on those of the strong. Your mere puny stripling, that winced at the least flourish of the rod, was passed by with indulgence; but the claims of justice were satisfied by inflicting a double portion on some little, tough, wrong-headed, broad-skirted Dutch urchin, who sulked and swelled and grew dogged and sullen beneath the birch. All this he called "doing his duty" by their parents; and he never inflicted a chastisement without following it by the assurance, so consolatory to the smarting urchin, that "he would remember it, and thank him for it the longest day he had to live."

When school-hours were over, he was even the companion and playmate of the larger boys; and on holiday afternoons would convoy some of the smaller ones home, who happened to have pretty sisters, or good housewives for mothers, noted for the comforts of the cupboard. Indeed it behooved him to keep on good terms with his pupils. The revenue arising from his school was small, and would have been scarcely sufficient to furnish him with daily bread, for he was a huge feeder, and, though lank, had the dilating powers of an anaconda; but to help out his maintenance, he was, according to country custom in those parts, boarded and lodged at the houses of the farmers, whose children he instructed. With these he lived successively a week at a time; thus going the rounds of the neighborhood, with all his worldly effects tied up in a cotton handkerchief.

That all this might not be too onerous on the purses of his rustic patrons, who are apt to consider the costs of schooling a grievious burden, and schoolmasters as mere drones, he had various ways of rendering himself both useful and agreeable. He assisted the farmers occasionally in the lighter labors of their farms; helped to make hay; mended the fences; took the horses to water; drove the cows from pasture; and cut wood for the winter fire. He laid aside, too, all the dominant dignity and absolute sway with which he lorded it in his little empire, the school, and became wonderfully gentle and ingratiating. He found favor in the eyes of the mothers, by petting the children, particularly the youngest; and like the lion bold, which whilom so magnanimously the lamb did hold, he would sit with a child on one knee, and rock a cradle with his foot for whole hours together.

In addition to his other vocations, he was the singing-master of the neighborhood, and picked up many bright shillings by instructing the young folks in psalmody. It was a matter of no little vanity to him, on Sundays, to take his station in front of the church-gallery, with a band of chosen singers; where, in his own mind, he completely carried away the palm from the parson. Certain it is, his voice resounded far above all the rest of the congregation; and there are peculiar quavers still to be heard in that church, and which may even be heard half a mile off, quite to the opposite side of the mill-pond, on a still Sunday morning, which are said to be legitimately descended from the nose of Ichabod Crane. Thus, by divers little makeshifts in that ingenious way which is commonly denominated "by hook and by crook," the worthy pedagogue got on tolerably enough, and was thought, by all who understood nothing of the labor of headwork, to have a wonderfully easy life of it.

The schoolmaster is generally a man of some importance in the female circle of a rural neighborhood; being considered a kind of idle, gentleman-like personage, of vastly superior taste and accomplishments to the rough country swains, and, indeed, inferior in learning only to the parson. His appearance, therefore, is apt to occasion some little stir at the tea-table of a farmhouse, and the addition of a supernumerary dish of cakes or sweet-meats, or, peradventure, the parade of a silver tea-pot. Our man of letters, therefore, was peculiarly happy in the smiles of all the country damsels. How he would figure among them in the churchyard, between services on Sundays! gathering grapes for them from the wild vines that overrun the surrounding trees; reciting for their amusement all the epitaphs on the tombstones; or sauntering, with a whole bevy of them, along the banks of the adjacent mill-pond; while the more bashful country bumpkins hung sheepishly back, envying his superior elegance and address.

From his half itinerant life, also, he was a kind of travelling gazette, carrying the whole budget of local gossip from house to house: so that his appearance was always greeted with satisfaction. He was, moreover, esteemed by the women as a man of great erudition, for he had read several books quite through, and was a perfect master of Cotton Mather's *History of New England Witchcraft*, in which, by the way, he most firmly and potently believed.

He was, in fact, an odd mixture of small shrewdness and simple credulity. His appetite for the marvellous, and his powers of digesting it, were equally extraordinary; and both had been increased by his residence in this spellbound region. No tale was too gross or monstrous for his capacious swallow. It was often his delight, after his school was dismissed in the afternoon, to stretch himself on the rich bed of clover bordering the little brook that whimpered by his school-house, and there con over old Mather's direful tales, until the gathering dusk of the evening made the printed page a mere mist before his eyes. Then, as he wended his way, by swamp and stream, and awful woodland, to the farm-house where he happened to be quartered, every sound of nature, at that witching hour, fluttered his excited imagination; the moan of the whippoorwill* from the hill-side, the boding cry

*The whippoorwill is a bird which is only heard at night. It receives its name from its note, which is thought to resemble those words.

49

of the tree-toad, that harbinger of storm; the dreary hooting of the screech-owl, or the sudden rustling in the thicket of birds frightened from their roost. The fire-flies, too, which sparkled most vividly in the darkest places, now and then startled him, as one of uncommon brightness would stream across his path; and if, by chance, a huge blockhead of a beetle came winging his blundering flight against him, the poor varlet was ready to give up the ghost, with the idea that he was struck with a witch's token. His only resource on such occasions, either to drown thought or drive away evil spirits, was to sing psalm-tunes; and the good people of Sleepy Hollow, as they sat by their doors of an evening, were often filled with awe, at hearing his nasal melody, "in linkèd sweetness long drawn out," floating from the distant hill, or along the dusky road.

Another of his sources of fearful pleasure was, to pass long winter evenings with the old Dutch wives, as they sat spinning by the fire, with a row of apples roasting and spluttering along the hearth, and listen to their marvellous tales of ghosts and goblins, and haunted fields, and haunted brooks, and haunted bridges, and haunted houses, and particularly of the headless horseman, or Galloping Hessian of the Hollow, as they sometimes called him. He would delight them equally by his anecdotes of witchcraft, and the direful omens and portentous sights and sounds in the air, which prevailed in the earlier times of Connecticut; and would frighten them wofully with speculations upon comets and shooting-stars, and with the alarming fact that the world did absolutely turn round, and that they were half the time topsy-turvy!

But if there was a pleasure in all this, while snugly cuddling in the chimney-corner of a chamber that was all of a ruddy glow from the crackling wood-fire, and where, of course, no spectre dared to show his face, it was dearly purchased by the terrors of his subsequent walk homewards. What fearful shapes and shadows beset his path amidst the dim and ghastly glare of a snowy night! — With what wistful look did he eye every trembling ray of light streaming across the waste fields from some distant window! — How often was he appalled by some shrub covered with snow, which, like a sheeted spectre, beset his very path! — How often did he shrink with curdling awe at the sound of his own steps on a frosty crust beneath his feet; and dread to look over his shoulder, lest he should behold some uncouth being tramping close behind him! — and how often was he thrown into complete dismay by some rushing blast, howling among the trees, in the idea that it was the Galloping Hessian on one of his nightly scourings!

All these, however, were mere terrors of the night, phantoms of the mind that walk in darkness; and though he had seen many spectres in his time, and been more than once beset by Satan in divers shapes, in his lonely perambulations, yet daylight put an end to all these evils; and he would have passed a pleasant life of it, in despite of the devil and all his works, if his path had not been crossed by a being that causes more perplexity to mortal man than ghosts, goblins, and the whole race of witches put together, and that was — a woman.

Among the musical disciples who assembled, one evening in each week, to receive his instructions in psalmody, was Katrina Van Tassel, the daughter and only child of a substantial Dutch farmer. She was a blooming lass of fresh eighteen; plump as a partridge; ripe and melting and rosy-cheeked as one of her father's peaches, and universally famed, not merely for her beauty, but her vast expectations. She was withal a little of a coquette, as might be perceived even in her dress, which was a mixture of ancient and modern fashions, as most suited to set off her charms. She wore the ornaments of pure yellow gold, which her great-great-grandmother had brought over from Saardam; the tempting stomacher of the olden time; and withal a provokingly short petticoat, to display the prettiest foot and ankle in the country round.

Ichabod Crane had a soft and foolish heart towards the sex; and it is not to be wondered at that so tempting a morsel soon found favor in his eyes; more especially after he had visited her in her paternal mansion. Old Baltus Van Tassel was a perfect picture of a thriving, contented, liberal-hearted farmer. He seldom, it is true, sent either his eyes or his thoughts beyond the boundaries of his own farm; but within those everything was snug, happy, and well-conditioned. He was satisfied with his wealth, but not proud of it; and piqued himself upon the hearty abundance rather than the style in which he lived. His stronghold was situated on the banks of the Hudson, in one of those green, sheltered, fertile nooks in which the Dutch farmers are so fond of nestling. A great elm-tree spread its broad branches over it; at the foot of which bubbled up a spring of the softest and sweetest water, in a little well, formed of a barrel; and then stole sparkling away through the grass, to a neighboring brook, that bubbled along among alders and dwarf willows. Hard by the farm-house was a vast barn, that might have served for a church; every window and crevice of which seemed bursting forth with the treasures of the farm; the flail was busily resounding within it from morning till night; swallows and martins skimmed twittering about the eaves; and rows of pigeons, some with one eye turned up, as if watching the weather, some with their heads under their wings, or buried in their bosoms, and others swelling, and cooing, and bowing about their dames, were enjoying the sunshine on the roof. Sleek unwieldly porkers were grunting in the repose and abundance of their pens; whence sallied forth, now and then, troops of sucking pigs, as if to snuff the air. A stately squadron of snowy geese were riding in an adjoining pond, convoying whole fleets of ducks; regiments of turkeys were gobbling through the farm-yard, and guinea fowls fretting about it, like ill-tempered housewives, with their peevish discontented cry. Before the barn-door strutted the gallant cock, that pattern of a husband, a warrior, and a fine gentleman, clapping his burnished wings, and crowing in the pride and gladness of his heart — sometimes tearing up the earth with his feet, and then generously calling his ever-hungry family of wives and children to enjoy the rich morsel which he had discovered.

The pedagogue's mouth watered, as he looked upon this sumptuous promise of luxurious winter fare. In his devouring mind's eye he pictured to himself every roasting-pig running about with a pudding in his belly, and an apple in his mouth; the pigeons were snugly put to bed in a comfortable pie, and tucked in with a coverlet of crust; the geese were swimming in their own gravy; and the ducks pairing cosily in dishes, like snug married couples, with a decent competency of onion-sauce. In the porkers he saw carved out the future sleek side of bacon, and juicy relishing ham; not a turkey but he beheld daintily trussed up, with its gizzard under its wing, and, peradventure, a necklace of savory sausages; and even bright chanticleer himself lay sprawling on his back, in a side-dish, with uplifted claws, as if craving that quarter which his chivalrous spirit disdained to ask while living.

As the enraptured Ichabod fancied all this, and as he rolled his great green eyes over the fat meadow-lands, the rich fields of wheat, of rye, of buckwheat, and Indian corn, and the orchard burdened with ruddy fruit, which surrounded the warm tenement of Van Tassel, his heart yearned after the damsel who was to inherit these domains, and his imagination expanded with the idea how they might be readily turned into cash, and the money invested in immense tracts of wild land, and shingle palaces in the wilderness. Nay, his busy fancy already realized his hopes, and presented to him the blooming Katrina, with a whole family of children, mounted on the top of a wagon loaded with household trumpery, with pots and kettles dangling beneath; and he beheld himself bestriding a pacing mare, with a colt at her heels, setting out for Kentucky, Tennessee, or the Lord knows where.

When he entered the house, the conquest of his heart was complete. It was one of those spacious farm-houses, with high-ridged, but lowly-sloping roofs, built in the style handed down from the first Dutch settlers; the low projecting eaves forming a piazza along the front, capable of being closed up in bad weather. Under this were hung flails, harness, various utensils of husbandry, and nets for fishing in the neighboring river. Benches were built along the sides for summer use; and a great spinning-wheel at one end, and a churn at the other, showed the various uses to which this important porch might be devoted. From this piazza the wandering Ichabod entered the hall, which formed the centre of the mansion and the place of usual residence. Here, rows of resplendent pewter, ranged on a long dresser, dazzled his eyes. In one corner stood a huge bag of wool ready to be spun; in another a quantity of linsey-woolsey just from the loom; ears of Indian corn, and strings of dried apples and peaches, hung in gay festoons along the walls, mingled with the gaud of red peppers; and a door left ajar gave him a peep into the best parlor, where the claw-footed chairs and dark mahogany tables shone like mirrors; and irons, with their accompanying shovel and tongs, glistened from their covert of asparagus tops; mock-oranges and conch-shells decorated the mantel-piece; strings of various colored birds' eggs were suspended above it, a great ostrich egg was hung from the centre of the room, and a corner-cupboard, knowingly left open, displayed immense treasures of old silver and well-mended china.

From the moment Ichabod laid his eyes upon these regions of delight, the peace of his mind was at an end, and his only study was how to gain the affections of the peerless daughter of Van Tassel. In this enterprise, however, he had more real difficulties than generally fell to the lot of a knight-errant of yore, who seldom had anything but giants, enchanters, fiery dragons, and such like easily conquered adversaries, to contend with; and had to make his way merely through gates of iron and brass, and walls of adamant, to the castle-keep, where the lady of his heart was confined; all which he achieved as easily as a man would carve his way to the centre of a Christmas pie; and then the lady gave him her hand as a matter of course. Ichabod, on the contrary, had to win his way to the heart of a country coquette, beset with a labyrinth of whims and caprices, which were forever presenting new difficulties and impediments; and he had to encounter a host of fearful adversaries of real flesh and blood, the numerous rustic admirers, who beset every portal to her heart; keeping a watchful and angry eye upon each other, but ready to fly out in the common cause against any new competitor.

Among these the most formidable was a burly, roaring, roistering blade, of the name of Abraham, or, according to the Dutch abbreviation, Brom Van Brunt, the hero of the country round, which rang with his feats of strength and hardihood. He was broad-shouldered and double-jointed, with short, curly black hair, and a bluff but not un-pleasant countenance, having a mingled air of fun and arrogance. From his Herculean frame and great powers of limb, he had received the nickname of BROM BONES, by which he was universally known. He was famed for great knowledge and skill in horsemanship, being as dexterous on horse-back as a Tartar. He was foremost at all races and cockfights; and, with the ascendency which bodily strength acquires in rustic life, was the umpire in all disputes, setting his hat on one side, and giving his decisions with an air and tone admitting of no gainsay or appeal. He was always ready for either a fight or a frolic; but had more mischief than ill-will in his composition; and, with all his overbearing roughness, there was a strong dash of waggish good-humor at the bottom. He had three or four boon companions, who regarded him as their model, and at the head of whom he scoured the country, attending every scene of feud or merriment for miles round. In cold weather he was distinguished by a fur cap, sur-mounted with a flaunting fox's tail; and when the folks at a country gathering de-scried this well-known crest at a distance, whisking about among a squad of hard riders, they always stood by for a squall.

Sometimes his crew would be heard dashing along past the farm-houses at midnight, with whoop and halloo, like a troop of Don Cossacks; and the old dames, startled out of their sleep, would listen for a moment till the hurry-scurry had clattered by, and then exclaim, "Ay, there goes Brom Bones and his gang!" The neighbors looked upon him with a mixture of awe, admiration, and good-will; and when any madcap prank, or rustic brawl, occurred in the vicinity, always shook their heads, and warranted Brom Bones was at the bottom of it.

This rantipole hero had for some time singled out the blooming Katrina for the object of his uncouth gallantries; and though his amorous toyings were something like the gentle caresses and endearments of a bear, yet it was whispered that she did not altogether discourage his hopes. Certain it is, his advances were signals for rival candidates to retire, who felt no inclination to cross a line in his amours; insomuch, that, when his horse was seen tied to Van Tassel's paling on a Sunday night, a sure sign that his master was courting, or, as it is termed, "sparking," within, all other suitors passed by in despair, and carried the war into other quarters.

Such was the formidable rival with whom

Ichabod Crane had to contend, and, considering all things, a stouter man than he would have shrunk from the competition, and a wiser man would have despaired. He had, however, a happy mixture of pliability and perseverance in his nature; he was in form and spirit like a supple-jack — yielding, but tough; though he bent, he never broke; and though he bowed beneath the slightest pressure yet, the moment it was away — jerk! he was as erect, and carried his head as high as ever.

To have taken the field openly against his rival would have been madness; for he was not a man to be thwarted in his amours, any more than that stormy lover, Achilles. Ichabod, therefore, made his advances in a quiet and gently insinuating manner. Under cover of his character of singing-master, he had made frequent visits at the farmhouse; not that he had anything to apprehend from the meddlesome interference of parents, which is so often a stumbling-block in the path of lovers. Balt Van Tassel was an easy, indulgent soul; he loved his daughter better even than his pipe, and, like a reasonable man and an excellent father, let her have her way in everything. His notable little wife, too, had enough to do to attend to her housekeeping and manage her poultry; for, as she sagely observed, ducks and geese are foolish things, and must be looked after, but girls can take care of themselves. Thus while the busy dame bustled about the house, or plied her spinning-wheel at one end of the piazza, honest Balt would sit smoking his evening pipe at the other, watching the achievements of a little wooden warrior, who, armed with a sword in each hand, was most valiantly fighting the wind on the pinnacle of the barn. In the meantime, Ichabod would carry on his suit with the daughter by the side of the spring under the great elm, or sauntering along in the twilight, — that hour so favorable to the lover's eloquence.

I profess not to know how women's hearts are wooed and won. To me they have always been matters of riddle and admiration. Some seem to have but one vulnerable point or door of access, while others have a thousand avenues, and may be captured in a thousand different ways. It is a great triumph of skill to gain the former, but a still greater proof of generalship to maintain possession of the latter, for the man must battle for his fortress at every door and window. He who wins a thousand common hearts is therefore entitled to some renown; but he who keeps undisputed sway over the heart of a coquette, is indeed a hero. Certain it is, this was not the case with the redoubt-able Brom Bones; and from the moment Ichabod Crane made his advances, the interests of the former evidently declined; his horse was no longer seen tied at the palings on Sunday nights, and a deadly feud gradually arose between him and the preceptor of Sleepy Hollow.

Brom, who had a degree of rough chivalry in his nature, would fain have carried matters to open warfare, and have settled their pretensions to the lady according to the mode of those most concise and simple reasoners, the knights-errant of yore — by single combat; but Ichabod was too conscious of the superior might of his adversary to enter the lists against him: he had overheard a boast of Bones, that he would "double the schoolmaster up, and lay him on a shelf of his own schoolhouse;" and he was too wary to give him an opportunity. There was something extremely provoking in this obstinately pacific system; it left Brom no alternative but to draw upon the funds of rustic waggery in his disposition, and to play off boorish practical jokes upon his rival. Ichabod became the object of whimsical persecution to Bones and his gang of rough riders. They harried his hitherto peaceful domains; smoked out his singing-school, by stopping up the chimney; broke into the school-house at night, in spite of its formidable fastenings of withe and window-stakes, and turned everything topsy-turvy: so that the poor schoolmaster began to think all the witches in the country held their meetings there. But what was still more annoying, Brom took opportunities of turning him into ridicule in presence of his mistress, and had a scoundrel dog whom he taught to whine in the most ludicrous manner, and introduced as a rival of Ichabod's to instruct her in psalmody.

In this way matters went on for some time, without producing any material effect on the relative situation of the contending powers. On a fine autumnal afternoon, Ichabod, in pensive mood, sat enthroned on the lofty stool whence he usually watched all the concerns of his little literary realm. In his hand he swayed a ferule, that sceptre of despotic power; the birch of justice reposed on three nails, behind the throne, a constant terror to evil-doers; while on the desk before him might be seen sundry contraband articles and prohibited weapons, detected upon the persons of idle urchins; such as half-munched apples, pop-guns, whirligigs, fly-cages, and whole legions of rampant little paper game-cocks. Apparently there had been some appalling act of justice recently inflicted, for his scholars were all busily intent upon their books, or slyly whispering behind them with one eye kept upon the master; and a kind of buzzing stillness reigned throughout the school-room. It was suddenly interrupted by the appearance of a negro, in tow-cloth jacket and trousers, a round-crowned fragment of a hat, like the cap of Mercury, and mounted on the back of a ragged, wild, half-broken colt, which he managed with a rope by way of halter. He came clattering up to the school-door with an invitation to Ichabod to attend a merry-making or "quilting frolic," to be held that evening at Mynheer Van Tassel's; and having delivered his message with that air of importance, and effort at fine language, which a negro is apt to display on petty embassies of the kind, he dashed over the brook, and was seen scampering away up the Hollow, full of the importance and hurry of his mission.

All was now bustle and hubbub in the late quiet school-room. The scholars were hurried through their lessons, without stopping at trifles; those who were nimble skipped over half with impunity, and those who were tardy had a smart application now and then in the rear, to quicken their speed, or help them over a tall word. Books were flung aside without being put away on the shelves, inkstands were overturned, benches thrown down, and the whole school was turned loose an hour before the usual time, bursting forth like a legion of young imps, yelping and racketing about the green, in joy at their early emancipation.

The gallant Ichabod now spent at least an extra half-hour at his toilet, brushing and furbishing up his best and indeed only suit of rusty black, and arranging his locks by a bit of broken looking-glass, that hung up in the school-house. That he might make his appearance before his mistress in the true style of a cavalier, he borrowed a horse from the farmer with whom he was domiciliated, a choleric old Dutchman, of the name of Hans Van Ripper, and, thus gallantly mounted, issued forth, like a knight-errant in quest of adventures. But it is meet I should, in the true spirit of romantic story, give some account of the looks and equipments of my hero and his steed. The animal he bestrode was a broken-down plough-horse, that had outlived almost everything but his viciousness. He was gaunt and shagged, with a ewe neck and a head like a hammer; his rusty mane and tail were tangled and knotted with burrs; one eye had lost its pupil, and was glaring and spectral; but the other had the gleam of a genuine devil in it. Still he must have had fire and mettle in his day, if we may judge from the name he bore of Gunpowder. He had, in fact, been a favorite steed of his master's, the choleric Van Ripper, who was a furious rider, and had infused, very probably, some of his own spirit into the animal; for, old and broken-down as he looked, there was more of the lurking devil in him than in any young filly in the country.

Ichabod was a suitable figure for such a steed. He rode with short stirrups, which brought his knees nearly up to the pommel of the saddle; his sharp elbows stuck out like grasshoppers'; he carried his whip perpendicularly in his hand, like a sceptre, and, as his horse jogged on, the motion of his arms was not unlike the flapping of a pair of wings. A small wool hat rested on the top of his nose, for so his scanty strip of forehead might be called; and the skirts of his black coat fluttered out almost to the horse's tail. Such was the appearance of Ichabod and his steed, as they shambled out of the gate of Hans Van Ripper, and it was altogether such an apparition as is seldom to be met with in broad daylight.

It was, as I have said, a fine autumnal day,

the sky was clear and nature wore that rich and golden livery which we always associate with the idea of abundance. The forests had put on their sober brown and yellow, while some trees of the tenderer kind had been nipped by the frosts into brilliant dyes of orange, purple, and scarlet. Streaming files of wild ducks began to make their appearance high in the air; the bark of the squirrel might be heard from the groves of beech and hickory nuts, and the pensive whistle of the quail at intervals from the neighboring stubble-field.

The small birds were taking their farewell banquets. In the fulness of their revelry, they fluttered, chirping and frolicking, from bush to bush, and tree to tree, capricious from the very profusion and variety around them. There was the honest cockrobin, the favorite game of stripling sportsmen, with its loud querulous notes; and the twittering blackbirds flying in sable clouds; and the golden-winged woodpecker, with his crimson crest, his broad black gorget, and splendid plumage; and the cedar-bird, with its red-tipt wings and yellow-tipt tail, and its little monteiro cap of feathers; and the blue jay, that noisy coxcomb, in his gay light-blue coat and white under-clothes, screaming and chattering, nodding and bobbing and bowing, and pretending to be on good terms with every songster of the grove.

As Ichabod jogged slowly on his way, his eye, ever open to every symptom of culinary abundance, ranged with delight over the treasures of jolly autumn. On all sides he beheld vast store of apples; some hanging in oppressive opulence on the trees; some gathered into baskets and barrels for the market; others heaped up in rich piles for the cider-press. Farther on he beheld great fields of Indian corn, with its golden ears peeping from their leafy coverts, and holding out the promise of cakes and hasty-pudding; and the yellow pumpkins lying beneath them, turning up their fair round bellies to the sun, and giving ample prospects of the most luxurious of pies; and anon he passed the fragrant buckwheat fields, breathing the odor of the bee-hive, and as he beheld them, soft anticipations stole over his mind of dainty slapjacks, well buttered, and garnished with honey or treacle, by the delicate little dimpled hand of Katrina Van Tassel.

Thus feeding his mind with many sweet thoughts and "sugared suppositions," he journeyed along the sides of a range of hills which look out upon some of the goodliest scenes of the mighty Hudson. The sun gradually wheeled his broad disk down into the west. The wide bosom of the Tappan Zee lay motionless and glossy, excepting that here and there a gentle undulation waved and prolonged the blue shadow of the distant mountain. A few amber clouds floated in the sky, without a breath of air to move them. The horizon was of a fine golden tint, changing gradually into a pure apple-green, and from that into the deep blue of the mid-heaven. A slanting ray lingered on the woody crests of the precipices that overhung some parts of the river, giving greater depth to the dark-gray and purple of their rocky sides. A sloop was loitering in the distance, dropping slowly down with the tide, her sail hanging uselessly against the mast; and as the reflection of the sky gleamed along the still water, it seemed as if the vessel was suspended in the air.

It was toward evening that Ichabod arrived at the castle of the Heer Van Tassel, which he found thronged with the pride and flower of the adjacent country. Old farmers, a spare leathern-faced race, in homespun coats and breeches, blue stockings, huge shoes, and magnificent pewter buckles. Their brisk withered little dames, in close crimped caps, long-waisted shortgowns, homespun petticoats, with scissors and pin-cushions, and gay calico pockets hanging on the outside. Buxom lasses, almost as anti-quated as their mothers, excepting where a straw hat, a fine ribbon, or perhaps a white frock, gave symptoms of city innovation. The sons, in short square-skirted coats with rows of stupendous brass buttons, and their hair generally queued in the fashion of the times, especially if they could procure an eel-skin for the purpose, it being esteemed, throughout the country, as a potent nour-isher and strengthener of the hair.

Brom Bones, however, was the hero of the scene, having come to the gathering on his favorite steed, Daredevil, a creature, like himself, full of mettle and mischief, and which no one but himself could manage. He was, in fact, noted for preferring vicious ani-mals, given to all kinds of tricks, which kept the rider in constant risk of his neck, for he held a tractable well-broken horse as un-worthy of a lad of spirit.

Fain would I pause to dwell upon the world of charms that burst upon the enrap-tured gaze of my hero, as he entered the state parlor of Van Tassel's mansion. Not those of the bevy of buxom lasses, with their luxurious display of red and white; but the ample charms of a genuine Dutch country tea-table, in the sumptuous time of autumn. Such heaped-up platters of cakes of various and almost indescribable kinds, known only to experienced Dutch housewives! There was the doughty doughnut, the tenderer oly koek, and the crisp and crumbling cruller; sweet cakes and short cakes, ginger-cakes and honey-cakes, and the whole family of cakes. And then there were apple-pies and peach-pies and pumpkin-pies; besides slices of ham and smoked beef; and moreover delectable dishes of preserved plums, and peaches, and pears, and quinces; not to mention broiled shad and roasted chickens; together with bowls of milk and cream, all mingled higgledy-piggledy, pretty much as I have enumerated them, with the motherly tea-pot sending up its clouds of vapor from the midst — Heaven bless the mark! I want breath and time to discuss this banquet as it deserves, and am too eager to get on with my story. Happily, Ichabod Crane was not in so great a hurry as his historian, but did ample justice to every dainty.

He was a kind and thankful creature, whose heart dilated in proportion as his skin was filled with good cheer; and whose spirits rose with eating as some men's do with drink. He could not help, too, rolling his large eyes round him as he ate, and chuckling with the possibility that he might one day be lord of all this scene of almost unimaginable luxury and splendor. Then, he thought, how soon he'd turn his back upon the old school-house; snap his fingers in the face of Hans Van Ripper, and every other niggardly patron, and kick any itinerant pedagogue out-of-doors that should dare to call him comrade!

Old Baltus Van Tassel moved about among his guests with a face dilated with content and good-humor, round and jolly as the harvest-moon. His hospitable attentions were brief, but expressive, being confined to a shake of the hand, a slap on the shoulder, a loud laugh, and a pressing invitation to "fall to, and help themselves."

And now the sound of the music from the common room, or hall, summoned to the dance. The musician was an old gray-headed negro, who had been the itinerant orchestra of the neighborhood for more than half a century. His instrument was as old and battered as himself. The greater part of the time he scraped on two or three strings, accompanying every movement of the bow with a motion of the head; bowing almost to the ground, and stamping with his foot whenever a fresh couple were to start.

Ichabod prided himself upon his dancing

as much as upon his vocal powers. Not a limb, not a fibre about him was idle; and to have seen his loosely hung frame in full motion, and clattering about the room, you would have thought Saint Vitus himself, that blessed patron of the dance, was figuring before you in person. He was the admiration of all the negroes; who, having gathered, of all ages and sizes, from the farm and the neighborhood, stood forming a pyramid of shining black faces at every door and window, gazing with delight at the scene, rolling their white eyeballs, and showing grinning rows of ivory from ear to ear. How could the flogger of urchins be otherwise than animated and joyous? the lady of his heart was his partner in the dance, and smiling graciously in reply to all his amorous oglings; while Brom Bones, sorely smitten with love and jealousy, sat brooding by himself in one corner.

When the dance was at an end, Ichabod was attracted to a knot of the sager folks, who, with old Van Tassel, sat smoking at one end of the piazza, gossiping over former times, and drawing out long stories about the war.

This neighborhood, at the time of which I am speaking, was one of those highly favored places which abound with chronicle and great men. The British and American line had run near it during the war; it had, therefore, been the scene of marauding, and infested with refugees, cow-boys, and all kinds of border chivalry. Just sufficient time has elapsed to enable each story-teller to dress up his tale with a little becoming fiction, and, in the indistinctness of his recollection, to make himself the hero of every exploit.

There was the story of Doffue Martling, a large blue-bearded Dutchman, who had nearly taken a British frigate with an old iron nine-pounder from a mud breastwork, only that his gun burst at the sixth discharge. And there was an old gentleman who shall be nameless, being too rich a mynheer to be lightly mentioned, who, in the battle of White Plains, being an excellent master of defence, parried a musketball with a small sword, insomuch that he absolutely felt it whiz round the blade, and glance off at the hilt; in proof of which he was ready at any time to show the sword, with the hilt a little bent. There were several more that had been equally great in the field, not one of whom but was persuaded that he had a considerable hand in bringing the war to a happy termination.

But all these were nothing to the tales of

ghosts and apparitions that succeeded. The neighborhood is rich in legendary treasures of the kind. Local tales and superstitions thrive best in these sheltered long-settled retreats; but are trampled underfoot by the shifting throng that forms the population of most of our country places. Besides, there is no encouragement for ghosts in most of our villages, for they have scarcely had time to finish their first nap, and turn themselves in their graves before their surviving friends have travelled away from the neighborhood; so that when they turn out at night to walk their rounds, they have no acquaintance left to call upon. This is perhaps the reason why we so seldom hear of ghosts, except in our long-established Dutch communities.

The immediate cause, however, of the prevalence of supernatural stories in these parts was doubtless owing to the vicinity of Sleepy Hollow. There was a contagion in the very air that blew from the haunted region; it breathed forth an atmosphere of dreams and fancies infecting all the land. Several of the Sleepy Hollow people were present at Van Tassel's and, as usual, were doling out their wild and wonderful legends. Many dismal tales were told about funeral trains, and mourning cries and wailings heard and seen about the great tree where the unfortunate Major André was taken, and which stood in the neighborhood. Some mention was made also of the woman in white, that haunted the dark glen at Raven Rock, and was often heard to shriek on winter nights before a storm, having perished there in the snow. The chief part of the stories, however, turned upon the favorite spectre of Sleepy Hollow, the headless horseman, who had been heard several times of late, patrolling the country; and, it was said, tethered his horse nightly among the graves in the churchyard.

The sequestered situation of this church seems always to have made it a favorite haunt of troubled spirits. It stands on a knoll, surrounded by locust-trees and lofty elms, from among which its decent white-washed walls shine modestly forth, like Christian purity beaming through the shades of retirement. A gentle slope descends from it to a silver sheet of water, bordered by high trees, between which, peeps may be caught at the blue hills of the Hudson. To look upon its grass-grown yard, where the sunbeams seem to sleep so quietly, one would think that there at least the dead might rest in peace. On one side of the church extends a wide woody dell, along which raves a large brook among broken rocks and trunks of fallen trees. Over a deep black part of the stream, not far from the church, was formerly thrown a wooden bridge; the road that led to it, and the bridge itself, were thickly shaded by overhanging trees, which cast a gloom about it, even in the daytime, but occasioned a fearful darkness at night. This was one of the favorite haunts of the headless horseman; and the place where he was most frequently encountered. The tale was told of old Brouwer, a most heretical disbeliever in ghosts, how he met the horseman returning from his foray into Sleepy Hollow, and was obliged to get up behind him; how they galloped over bush and brake, over hill and swamp, until they reached the bridge; when the horseman suddenly turned into a skeleton, threw old Brouwer into the brook, and sprang away over the tree-tops with a clap of thunder.

This story was immediately matched by a thrice marvellous adventure of Brom Bones, who made light of the galloping Hessian as an arrant jockey. He affirmed that, on returning one night from the neighboring village of Sing Sing, he had been overtaken by this midnight trooper; that he had offered to race with him for a bowl of punch, and should have won it too, for Daredevil beat the goblin horse all hollow, but, just as they came to the church bridge, the Hessian bolted, and vanished in a flash of fire.

All these tales, told in that drowsy undertone with which men talk in the dark, the countenances of the listeners only now and then receiving a casual gleam from the glare of a pipe, sank deep in the mind of Ichabod. He repaid them in kind with large extracts from his invaluable author, Cotton Mather, and added many marvellous events that had taken place in his native State of Connecticut, and fearful sights which he had seen in his nightly walks about the Sleepy Hollow.

The revel now gradually broke up. The old farmers gathered together their families in their wagons, and were heard for some time rattling along the hollow roads, and over the distant hills. Some of the damsels mounted on pillions behind their favorite swains, and their light-hearted laughter, mingling with the clatter of hoofs, echoed along the silent woodlands, sounding fainter and fainter until they gradually died away — and the late scene of noise and frolic was all silent and deserted. Ichabod only lingered behind, according to the custom of country lovers, to have a *tête-à-tête* with the heiress, fully convinced that he was now on the high road to success. What passed at this interview I will not pretend to say, for in fact I do not know. Something, however, I fear me, must have gone wrong, for he certainly sallied forth, after no very great interval, with an air quite desolate and chop-fallen. — Oh, these women! these women! Could that girl have been playing off any of her coquettish tricks? — Was her encouragement of the poor pedagogue all a mere sham to secure her conquest of his rival? — Heaven only knows, not I! — Let it suffice to say, Ichabod stole forth with the air of one who had been sacking a hen-roost, rather than a fair lady's heart. Without looking to the right or left to notice the scene of rural wealth on which he had so often gloated, he went straight to the stable, and with several hearty cuffs and kicks, roused his steed most uncourteously from the comfortable quarters in which he was soundly sleeping, dreaming of mountains of corn and oats, and whole valleys of timothy and clover.

It was the very witching time of night that Ichabod, heavy-hearted and crestfallen, pursued his travel homewards, along the sides of the lofty hills which rise above Tarry Town, and which he had traversed so cheerily in the afternoon. The hour was as dismal as himself. Far below him, the Tappan Zee spread its dusky and indistinct waste of waters, with here and there the tall mast of a sloop riding quietly at anchor under the land. In the dead hush of midnight he could even hear the barking of the watch-dog from the opposite shore of the Hudson; but it was so vague and faint as only to give an idea of his distance from this faithful companion of man. Now and then, too, the long-drawn crowing of a cock, accidentally awakened, would sound far, far off, from some farm-house away among the hills — but it was like a dreaming sound in his ear. No signs of life occurred near him, but occasionally the melancholy chirp of a cricket, or perhaps the gutteral twang of a bull-frog, from a neighboring marsh, as if sleeping uncomfortably, and turning suddenly in his bed.

All the stories of ghosts and goblins that he had heard in the afternoon, now came crowding upon his recollection. The night grew darker and darker; the stars seemed to sink deeper in the sky, and driving clouds occasionally hid them from his sight. He had never felt so lonely and dismal. He was, moreover, approaching the very place where many of the scenes of the ghost-stories had been laid. In the centre of the road stood an enormous tulip-tree, which towered like a giant above all the other trees of the neighborhood, and formed a kind of landmark. Its limbs were gnarled, and fantastic, large enough to form trunks for ordinary trees, twisting down almost to the earth, and rising again into the air. It was connected with the tragical story of the unfortunate André, who had been taken prisoner hard by; and was universally known by the name of Major André's tree. The common people regarded it with a mixture of respect and superstition, partly out of sympathy for the fate of its ill-starred namesake, and partly from the tales of strange sights and doleful lamentations told concerning it.

As Ichabod approached this fearful tree, he began to whistle: he thought his whistle was answered, — it was but a blast sweeping sharply through the dry branches. As he approached a little nearer, he thought he saw something white, hanging in the midst of the tree, — he paused and ceased whistling; but on looking more narrowly, perceived that it was a place where the tree had been scathed by lightning, and the white wood laid bare. Suddenly he heard a groan, — his teeth chattered and his knees smote against the saddle: it was but the rubbing of one huge bough upon another, as they were swayed about by the breeze. He passed the tree in safety; but new perils lay before him.

About two hundred yards from the tree a small brook crossed the road, and ran into a marshy and thickly wooded glen, known by the name of Wiley's swamp. A few rough logs, laid side by side, served for a bridge over this stream. On that side of the road where the brook entered the wood, a group of oaks and chestnuts, matted thick with wild grape-vines, threw a cavernous gloom over it. To pass this bridge was the severest trial. It was at this identical spot that the unfortunate André was captured, and under the covert of those chestnuts and vines were the sturdy yeomen concealed who surprised him. This has ever since been considered a haunted stream, and fearful are the feelings of the school boy who has to pass it alone after dark.

As he approached the stream, his heart began to thump; he summoned up, however, all his resolution, gave his horse half a score of kicks in the ribs, and attempted to dash briskly across the bridge; but instead of starting forward, the perverse old animal made a lateral movement, and ran broadside against the fence. Ichabod, whose fears increased with the delay, jerked the reins on the other side, and kicked lustily with the contrary foot: it was all in vain; his steed started, it is true, but it was only to plunge to the opposite side of the road into a thicket of brambles and alder bushes. The schoolmaster now bestowed both whip and heel upon the starveling ribs of old Gunpowder, who dashed forward, snuffling and snorting, but came to a stand just by the bridge, with a suddenness that had nearly sent his rider sprawling over his head. Just at this moment a plashy tramp by the side of the bridge caught the sensitive ear of Ichabod. In the dark shadow of the grove, on the margin of the brook, he beheld something huge, misshapen, black, and towering. It stirred not, but seemed gathered up in the gloom, like some gigantic monster ready to spring upon the traveller.

The hair of the affrighted pedagogue rose upon his head with terror. What was to be done? To turn and fly was now too late; and besides, what chance was there of escaping ghost or goblin, if such it was, which could ride upon the wings of the wind? Summoning up, therefore, a show of courage, he demanded in stammering accents — "Who are you?" He received no reply. He repeated his demand in a still more agitated voice. Still there was no answer. Once more he cudgelled the sides of the inflexible Gunpowder, and, shutting his eyes, broke forth with involuntary fervor into a psalm-tune.

Just then the shadowy object of alarm put itself in motion, and, with a scramble and a bound, stood at once in the middle of the road. Though the night was dark and dismal, yet the form of the unknown might now in some degree be ascertained. He appeared to be a horseman of large dimensions, and mounted on a black horse of powerful frame. He made no offer of molestation or sociability, but kept aloof on one side of the road, jogging along on the blind side of old Gunpowder, who had now got over his fright and waywardness.

Ichabod, who had no relish for this strange midnight companion, and bethought himself of the adventure of Brom Bones with the Galloping Hessian, now quickened his steed, in hopes of leaving him behind. The stranger, however, quickened his horse to an equal pace. Ichabod pulled up, and fell into a walk, thinking to lag behind, — the other did the same. His heart began to sink within him; he endeavored to resume his psalm-tune, but his parched tongue clove to the roof of his mouth, and he could not utter a stave. There was something in the moody and dogged silence of this pertinacious companion, that was mysterious and appalling. It was soon fearfully accounted for. On mounting a rising ground, which brought the figure of his fellow-traveller in relief against the sky, gigantic in height, and muffled in a cloak, Ichahod was horror-struck, on perceiving that he was headless! — but his horror was still more increased, on observing that the head, which should have rested on his shoulders, was carried before him on the pommel of the saddle: his terror rose to desperation; he rained a shower of kicks and blows upon Gunpowder, hoping, by a sudden movement, to give his companion the slip, — but the spectre started full jump with him. Away then they dashed, through thick and thin; stones flying, and sparks flashing at every bound. Ichabod's flimsy garments fluttered in the air, as he stretched his long lank body away over his horse's head, in the eagerness of his flight.

They had now reached the road which turns off to Sleepy Hollow; but Gunpowder, who seemed possessed with a demon, instead of keeping up it, made an opposite turn, and plunged headlong downhill to the left. This road leads through a sandy hollow, shaded by trees for about a quarter of a mile, where it crosses the bridge famous in goblin story, and just beyond swells the green knoll on which stands the whitewashed church,

As yet the panic of the steed had given his

unskilful rider an apparent advantage in the chase; but just as he had got half-way through the hollow, the girths of the saddle gave way, and he felt it slipping from under him. He seized it by the pommel, and endeavored to hold it firm, but in vain; and had just time to save himself by clasping old Gunpowder round the neck, when the saddle fell to the earth, and he heard it trampled underfoot by his pursuer. For a moment, the terror of Hans Van Ripper's wrath passed across his mind — for it was his Sunday saddle; but this was no time for petty fears; the goblin was hard on his haunches; and (unskilful rider that he was!) he had much ado to maintain his seat; sometimes slipping on one side, sometimes on another, and sometimes jolted on the high ridge of his horse's backbone, with a violence that he verily feared would cleave him asunder.

An opening in the trees now cheered him with the hopes that the church-bridge was at hand. The wavering reflection of a silver star in the bosom of the brook told him that he was not mistaken. He saw the walls of the church dimly glaring under the trees beyond. He recollected the place where Brom Bones' ghostly competitor had disappeared. "If I can but reach that bridge," thought

Ichabod, "I am safe." Just then he heard the black steed panting and blowing close behind him; he even fancied that he felt his hot breath. Another convulsive kick in the ribs, and old Gunpowder sprang upon the bridge; he thundered over the resounding planks; he gained the opposite side; and now Ichabod cast a look behind to see if his pursuer should vanish, according to rule, in a flash of fire and brimstone. Just then he saw the goblin rising in his stirrups, and in the very act of hurling his head at him. Ichabod endeavored to dodge the horrible missile, but too late. It encountered his cranium with a tremendous crash, — he was tumbled headlong into the dust, and Gunpowder, the black steed, and the goblin rider, passed by like a whirlwind.

The next morning the old horse was found without his saddle, and with the bridle under his feet, soberly cropping the grass at his master's gate. Ichabod did not make his appearance at breakfast; — dinner-hour came, but no Ichabod. The boys assembled at the school-house, and strolled idly about the banks of the brook; but no schoolmaster. Hans Van Ripper now began to feel some uneasiness about the fate of poor Ichabod, and his saddle. An inquiry was set on foot, and after diligent investigation they came upon his traces. In one part of the road leading to the church was found the saddle trampled in the dirt; the tracks of horses' hoofs deeply dented in the road, and evidently at furious speed, were traced to the bridge, beyond which, on the bank of a broad part of the brook, where the water ran deep and black, was found the hat of the unfortunate Ichabod, and close beside it a shattered pumpkin.

The brook was searched, but the body of the schoolmaster was not to be discovered. Hans Van Ripper, as executor of his estate, examined the bundle which contained all his worldly effects. They consisted of two shirts and a half; two stocks for the neck; a pair or two of worsted stockings, an old pair of corduroy small-clothes; a rusty razor; a book of psalm-tunes, full of dogs' ears; and a broken pitch-pipe. As to the books and furniture of the school-house, they belonged to the community, excepting Cotton Mather's *History of Witchcraft*, a *New England Almanac*, and a book of dreams and fortune-telling; in which last was a sheet of foolscap much scribbled and blotted in several fruitless attempts to make a copy of verses in honor of the heiress of Van Tassel. These magic books and the poetic scrawl were forthwith consigned to the flames by Hans

Van Ripper; who from that time forward determined to send his children no more to school; observing, that he never knew any good come of this same reading and writing. Whatever money the schoolmaster possessed, and he had received his quarter's pay but a day or two before, he must have had about his person at the time of his disappearance.

The mysterious event caused much speculation at the church on the following Sunday. Knots of gazers and gossips were collected in the churchyard, at the bridge, and at the spot where the hat and pumpkin had been found. The stories of Brouwer, of Bones, and a whole budget of others, were called to mind; and when they had diligently considered them all, and compared them with the symptoms of the present case, they shook their heads, and came to the conclusion that Ichabod had been carried off by the Galloping Hessian. As he was a bachelor, and in nobody's debt, nobody troubled his head any more about him. The school was removed to a different quarter of the Hollow, and another pedagogue reigned in his stead.

It is true, an old farmer, who had been down to New York on a visit several years after, and from whom this account of the ghastly adventure was received, brought home the intelligence that Ichabod Crane was still alive; that he had left the neighborhood, partly through fear of the goblin and Hans Van Ripper, and partly in mortification at having been suddenly dismissed by the heiress; that he had changed his quarters to a distant part of the country; had kept school and studied law at the same time, had been admitted to the bar, turned politician, electioneered, written for the newspapers, and finally had been made a justice of the Ten Pound Court. Brom Bones too, who shortly after his rival's disappearance conducted the blooming Katrina in triumph to the altar, was observed to look exceedingly knowing whenever the story of Ichabod was related, and always burst into a hearty laugh at the mention of the pumpkin; which led some to suspect that he knew more about the matter than he chose to tell.

The old country wives, however, who are the best judges of these matters, maintain to this day that Ichabod was spirited away by supernatural means; and it is a favorite story often told about the neighborhood round the winter evening fire. The bridge became more than ever an object of superstitious awe, and that may be the reason why the road has been altered of late years, so as to approach the church by the border of the millpond. The school-house, being deserted, soon fell to decay, and was reported to be haunted by the ghost of the unfortunate pedagogue; and the plough-boy, loitering homeward of a still summer evening, has often fancied his voice at a distance, chanting a melancholy psalm-tune, among the tranquil solitudes of Sleepy Hollow.

POSTSCRIPT,
Found in the Handwriting of Mr. Knickerbocker.

The preceding Tale is given, almost in the precise words in which I beard it related at a Corporation meeting of the ancient city of Manhattoes, at which were present many of its sagest and most illustrious burghers. The narrator was a pleasant, shabby, gentlemanly old fellow, in pepper-and-salt clothes, with a sadly humorous face; and one whom I strongly suspected of being poor, — he made such efforts to be entertaining. When his story was concluded, there was much laughter and approbation, particularly from two or three deputy aldermen, who had been asleep the greater part of the time. There was, however, one tall, dry-looking old gentleman, with beetling eyebrows, who maintained a grave and rather severe face throughout; now and then folding his arms, inclining his head, and looking down upon the floor, as if turning a doubt over in his mind. He was one of your wary men, who never laugh, but on good grounds — when they have reason and the law on their side. When the mirth of the rest of the company had subsided and silence was restored, he leaned one arm on the elbow of his chair, and sticking the other akimbo, demanded, with a slight but exceedingly sage motion of the head, and contraction of the brow, what was the moral of the story, and what it went to prove?

The story-teller, who was just putting a glass of wine to his lips, as a refreshment after his toils, paused for a moment, looked at his inquirer with an air of infinite deference, and, lowering the glass slowly to the table, observed, that the story was intended most logically to prove:

"There is no situation in life but has its advantages and pleasures — provided we will but take a joke as we find it;

"That, therefore, he that runs races with goblin troopers is likely to have rough riding of it.

"*Ergo,* for a country schoolmaster to be

refused the hand of a Dutch heiress, is a certain step to high preferment in the state."

The cautious old gentleman knit his brows tenfold closer after this explanation, being sorely puzzled by ratiocination of the syllogism; while, methought, the one in pepper-and-salt eyed him with something of a triumphant leer. At length he observed, that all this was very well, but still he thought the story a little on the extravagant — there were one or two points on which he had his doubts.

"Faith, sir," replied the story-teller, "as to that matter, I don't believe one half of it myself."

D.K.

From *The Sketch* Book

The Club
of Queer Fellows

I think it was the very next evening that, in coming out of Covent Garden Theatre with my eccentric friend Buckthorne, he proposed to give me another peep at life and character. Finding me willing for any research of the kind, he took me through a variety of the narrow courts and lanes about Covent Garden, until we stopped before a tavern, from which we heard the bursts of merriment of a jovial party. There would be a loud peal of laughter, then an interval, then another peal, as if a prime wag were telling a story. After a little while there was a song, and at the close of each stanza a hearty roar, and a vehement thumping on the table.

"This is the place," whispered Buckthorne; "it is the club of Queer Fellows, a great resort of the small wits, third-rate ac-

and newspaper critics of the theatres. .iy one can go in on paying a sixpence at the bar for the use of the club."

We entered, therefore, without ceremony, and took our seats at a lone table, in a dusky corner of the room. The club was assembled round a table on which stood beverages of various kinds, according to the tastes of the individuals. The members were a set of queer fellows indeed; but what was my surprise on recognizing, in the prime wit of the meeting, the poor-devil author whom I had remarked at the booksellers' dinner for his promising face and his complete taciturnity. Matters, however, were entirely changed with him. There he was a mere cipher; here he was lord of the ascendant, the choice spirit, the dominant genius. He sat at the head of the table with his hat on, and an eye beaming even more luminously than his nose. He had a quip and a fillip for every one, and a good thing on every occasion. Nothing could be said or done without eliciting a spark from him: and I solemnly declare I have heard much worse wit even from noblemen. His jokes, it must be confessed, were rather wet, but they suited the circle over which he presided. The company were in that maudlin mood, when a little wit goes a great way. Every time he opened his lips there was sure to be a roar; and even sometimes before he had time to speak.

We were fortunate enough to enter in time for a glee composed by him expressly for the club, and which he sung with two boon companions, who would have been worthy subjects for Hogarth's pencil. As they were each provided with a written copy, I was enabled to procure the reading of it.

"Merrily, merrily, push round the glass,
   And merrily troll the glee,
For he who won't drink till he wink is a ass,
   So, neighbor, I drink to thee.

"Merrily, merrily, fuddle thy nose,
   Until it right rosy shall be;
For a jolly red nose, I speak under the rose,
   Is a sign of good company."

We waited until the party broke up, and no one but the wit remained. He sat at the table with his legs stretched under it, and wide apart; his hands in his breeches-pockets; his head drooped upon his breast; and gazing with lack-lustre countenance on an empty tankard. His gaiety was gone, his fire completely quenched.

My companion approached, and startled him from his fit of brown study, introducing himself on the strength of their having dined together at the booksellers.

"By the way," said he, "it seems to me I have seen you before; your face is surely that of an old acquaintance, though for the life of me I cannot tell where I have known you."

"Very likely," replied he, with a smile; "many of my old friends have forgotten me. Though, to tell the truth, my memory in this instance is as bad as your own. If, however, it will assist your recollection in any way, my name is Thomas Dribble, at your service. "

"What! Tom Dribble, who was at old Birchell's school in Warwickshire?"

"The same," said the other, coolly.

"Why, then, we are old schoolmates, though it's no wonder you don't recollect me. I was your junior by several years; don't you recollect little Jack Buckthorne?"

Here there ensued a scene of school-fellow recognition, and a world of talk about old school-times and school-pranks. Mr. Dribble ended by observing, with a heavy sigh, "that times were sadly changed since those days."

"Faith, Mr. Dribble," said I, "you seem quite a different man here from what you were at dinner. I had no idea that you had so much stuff in you. There you were all silence, but here you absolutely keep the table in a roar."

"Ah! my dear sir," replied he, with a shake of the head, and a shrug of the shoulder, "I am a mere glow-worm. I never shine by daylight. Besides, it's a hard thing for a poor devil of an author to shine at the table of a rich bookseller. Who do you think would laugh at anything I could say, when I had some of the current wits of the day about me? But here, though a poor devil, I am among still poorer devils than myself; men who look up to me as a man of letters, and a *belle-espirit,* and all my jokes pass as sterling gold from the mint."

"You surely do yourself injustice, sir," said I; "I have certainly heard more good things from you this evening than from any of those *beaux-espirits* by whom you appear to have been so daunted."

"Ah, sir! but they have luck on their side; they are in the fashion — there's nothing like being in fashion. A man that has once got his character up for a wit is always sure of a laugh, say what he may. He may utter as much nonsense as he pleases, and all will pass current. No one stops to question the coin of a rich man; but a poor devil cannot pass off either a joke or a guinea, without its being examined on both sides. Wit and coin are always doubted with a threadbare coat.

"For my part," continued he, giving his hat a twitch a little more on one side, — "for my part, I hate your fine dinners; there's nothing, sir, like the freedom of a chop-house. I'd rather, any time, have my steak and tankard among my own set, than drink claret and eat venison with your cursed civil, elegant company, who never laugh at a good joke from a poor devil for fear of its being vulgar. A good joke grows in a wet soil; it flourishes in low places, but wither on your d — d high, dry grounds. I once kept high company, sir, until I nearly ruined myself; I grew so dull, and vapid, and genteel. Nothing saved me but being arrested by my landlady, and thrown into prison; where a course of catch-clubs, eight-penny ale, and poor-devil company, manured my mind, and brought it back to itself again."

As it was now growing late, we parted for the evening, though I felt anxious to know more of this practical philosopher. I was glad, therefore, when Buckthorne proposed to have another meeting, to talk over old school-times, and inquired his schoolmate's address. The latter seemed at first a little shy of naming his lodgings; but suddenly, as-suming an air of hardihood — "Green-arbor

Court, sir," exclaimed he — "Number —— in Green-arbor Court. You must know the place. Classic ground, sir, classic ground! It was there Goldsmith wrote his *Vicar of Wakefield* — I always like to live in literary haunts."

I was amused with this whimsical apology for shabby quarters. On our way homeward, Buckthorne assured me that this Dribble had been the prime wit and great wag of the school in their boyish days, and one of those unlucky urchins denominated bright geniuses. As he perceived me curious respecting his old schoolmate, he promised to take me with him in his proposed visit to Green-arbor Court.

A few mornings afterward he called upon me, and we set forth on our expedition. He led me through a variety of singular alleys, and courts, and blind passages; for he appeared to be perfectly versed in all the intricate geography of the metropolis. At length we came out upon Fleet Market, and traversing it, turned up a narrow street to the bottom of a long, steep flight of stone steps, called Break-neck Stairs. These, he told me, led up to Green-arbor Court, and that down them poor Goldsmith might many a time have risked his neck. When we entered the court, I could not but smile to think in what out-of-the-way corners genius produces her bantlings! And the muses, those capricious dames, who, forsooth, so often refuse to visit palaces, and deny a single smile to votaries in splendid studies, and gilded drawing-rooms, — what holes and burrows will they frequent to lavish their favors on some ragged disciple!

This Green-arbor Court I found to be a small square, surrounded by tall and miserable houses, the very intestines of which seemed turned inside out, to judge from the old garments and frippery fluttering from every window. It appeared to be a region of washerwomen, and lines were stretched about the little square, on which clothes were dangling to dry.

Just as we entered the square, a scuffle took place between two viragoes about a disputed right to a wash-tub, and immediately the whole community was in a hub-bub. Heads in mob-caps popped out of every window, and such a clamor of tongues ensued, that I was fain to stop my ears. Every amazon took part with one or other of the disputants, and brandished her arms, dripping with soap-suds, and fired away from her window as from the embrazure of a fortress; while the swarms of children nestled and cradled in every procreant chamber of this hive, waking with the noise, set up their shrill pipes to swell the general concert.

Poor Goldsmith! what a time he must have had of it, with his quiet disposition and nervous habits, penned up in this den of noise and vulgarity! How strange that, while every sight and sound was sufficient to embitter the heart, and fill it with misanthropy, his pen should be dropping the honey of Hybla! Yet it is more than probable that he drew many of his inimitable pictures of low life from the scenes which surrounded him in this abode. The circumstance of Mrs. Tibbs being obliged to wash her husband's two shirts in a neighbor's house, who refused to lend her wash-tub, may have been no sport of fancy, but a fact passing under his own eye. His landlady may have sat for the picture, and Beau Tibbs's scanty wardrobe have been a *fac-simile* of his own.

It was with some difficulty that we found our way to Dribble's lodgings. They were up two pair of stairs, in a room that looked upon the court; and when we entered, he was seated on the edge of his bed, writing at a broken table. He received us, however, with a free, open, poor-devil air, that was irresistible. It is true he did at first appear slightly confused; buttoned up his waistcoat a little higher, and tucked in a stray frill of linen. But he recollected himself in an instant; gave a half-swagger, half-leer, as he stepped forth to receive us; drew a three-legged stool for Mr. Buckthorne; pointed me to a lumbering old damask chair, that looked like a dethroned monarch in exile; and bade us welcome to his garret.

We soon got engaged in conversation. Buckthorne and he had much to say about early school-scenes; and as nothing opens a man's heart more than recollections of the kind, we soon drew from him a brief outline of his literary career.

The Devil
and Tom Walker

A few miles from Boston in Massachusetts, there is a deep inlet, winding several miles into the interior of the country from Charles Bay, and terminating in a thickly-wooded swamp or morass. On one side of this inlet is a beautiful dark grove; on the opposite side the land rises abruptly from the water's edge into a high ridge, on which grow a few scattered oaks of great age and immense size. Under one of these gigantic trees, according to old stories, there was a great amount of treasure buried by Kidd the pirate. The inlet allowed a facility to bring the money in a boat secretly and at night to the very foot of the hill; the elevation of the place permitted a good lookout to be kept that no one was at hand; while the remarkable trees formed good landmarks by which the place might easily be found again. The old stories add, moreover, that the devil presided at the hiding of the money, and took it under his guardianship; but this, it is well known, he always does with buried treasure, particularly when it has been ill-gotten. Be that as it may, Kidd never returned to recover his wealth; being shortly after seized at Boston, sent out to England, and there hanged for a pirate.

About the year 1727, just at the time that earthquakes were prevalent in New England, and shook many tall sinners down upon their knees, there lived near this place a meagre, miserly fellow, of the name of Tom Walker. He had a wife as miserly as himself: they were so miserly that they even conspired to cheat each other. Whatever the woman could lay hands on, she hid away; a hen could not cackle but she was on the alert to secure the new-laid egg. Her husband was continually prying about to detect her secret hoards, and many and fierce were the conflicts that took place about what ought to have been common property. They lived in a forlorn-looking house that stood alone, and had an air of starvation. A few straggling savin-trees, emblems of sterility, grew near it; no smoke ever curled from its chimney; no traveller stopped at its door. A miserable horse, whose ribs were as articulate as the bars of a gridiron, stalked about a field, where a thin carpet of moss, scarcely covering the ragged beds of pudding-stone, tantalized and balked his hunger; and sometimes he would lean his head over the fence, look piteously at the passer-by, and seem to petition deliverance from this land of famine.

The house and its inmates had altogether a bad name. Tom's wife was a tall termagant, fierce of temper, loud of tongue, and strong of arm. Her voice was often heard in wordy warfare with her husband; and his face sometimes showed signs that their conflicts were not confined to words. No one ventured, however, to interfere between them. The lonely wayfarer shrunk within himself at the horrid clamor and clapper-clawing; eyed the den of discord askance; and hurried on his way, rejoicing, if a bachelor, in his celibacy.

One day that Tom Walker had been to a distant part of the neighborhood, he took what he considered a short cut homeward, through the swamp. Like most short cuts, it was an ill-chosen route. The swamp was thickly grown with great gloomy pines and hemlocks, some of them ninety feet high, which made it dark at noonday, and a retreat for all the owls of the neighborhood. It was full of pits and quagmires, partly covered with weeds and mosses, where the green surface often betrayed the traveller into a gulf of black, smothering mud: there were also dark and stagnant pools, the abodes of the tadpole, the bull-frog, and the water-snake; where the trunks of pines and hemlocks lay half drowned, half rotting, looking like alligators sleeping in the mire.

Tom had long been picking his way cautiously through this treacherous forest; stepping from tuft to tuft of rushes and roots, which afforded precarious footholds among deep sloughs; or pacing carefully, like a cat, along the prostrate trunks of trees; startled now and then by the sudden screaming of the bittern, or the quacking of wild duck rising on the wing from some solitary pool. At length he arrived at a firm piece of ground, which ran out like a peninsula into the deep bosom of the swamp. It had been one of the strongholds of the Indians during their wars with the first colonists. Here they had thrown up a kind of fort, which they had looked upon as almost impregnable, and had used as a place of refuge for their squaws and children. Nothing remained of the old Indian fort but a few embankments, gradually sinking to the level of the surrounding earth, and already overgrown in part by oaks and other forest trees, the foliage of which formed a contrast to the dark pines and hemlocks of the swamp.

It was late in the dusk of evening when Tom Walker reached the old fort, and he paused there awhile to rest himself. Any one but he would have felt unwilling to linger in this lonely, melancholy place, for the common people had a bad opinion of it, from the stories handed down from the time of the Indian wars; when it was asserted that the savages held incantations here, and made sacrifices to the evil spirit.

Tom Walker, however, was not a man to be troubled with any fears of the kind. He reposed himself for some time on the trunk of a fallen hemlock, listening to the boding cry of the tree-toad, and delving with his walking-staff into a mound of black mould at his feet. As he turned up the soil unconsciously, his staff struck against something hard. He raked it out of the vegetable mould, and lo! a cloven skull, with an Indian tomahawk buried deep in it, lay before him. The rust on the weapon showed the time that had elapsed since this death-blow had been given. It was a dreary memento of the fierce struggle that had taken place in this last foothold of the Indian warriors.

"Humph!" said Tom Walker, as he gave it a kick to shake the dirt from it.

"Let that skull alone!" said a gruff voice. Tom lifted up his eyes, and beheld a great black man seated directly opposite him, on the stump of a tree. He was exceedingly surprised, having neither heard nor seen any one approach; and he was still more perplexed on observing, as well as the gathering gloom would permit, that the stranger was neither negro nor Indian. It is true he was dressed in a rude half Indian garb, and had a red belt or sash swathed round his body; but his face was neither black nor copper-color, but swarthy and dingy, and begrimed with soot, as if he had been accustomed to toil among fires and forges. He had a shock of coarse black hair, that stood out from his head in all directions, and bore an axe on his shoulder.

He scowled for a moment at Tom with a pair of great red eyes.

"What are you doing on my grounds?" said the black man, with a hoarse, growling voice.

"Your grounds!" said Tom, with a sneer, "no more your grounds than mine; they belong to Deacon Peabody."

"Deacon Peabody be d——d," said the stranger, "as I flatter myself he will be, if he does not look more to his own sins and less to those of his neighbors. Look yonder, and see how Deacon Peabody is faring."

Tom looked in the direction that the stranger pointed, and beheld one of the great trees, fair and flourishing without, but rotten at the core, and saw that it had been nearly hewn through, so that the first high wind was likely to blow it down. On the bark of the tree was scored the name of Deacon Peabody, an eminent man, who had waxed wealthy by driving shrewd bargains with the Indians. He now looked around, and found most of the tall trees marked with the name of some great man of the colony, and all more or less scored by the axe. The one on which he had been seated, and which had evidently just been hewn down, bore the name of Crowninshield; and he recollected a mighty rich man of that name, who made a vulgar display of wealth, which it was whispered he had acquired by buccaneering.

"He's just ready for burning!" said the black man, with a growl of triumph. "You see I am likely to have a good stock of firewood for winter."

"But what right have you," said Tom, "to cut down Deacon Peabody's timber?"

"The right of a prior claim," said the other. "This woodland belonged to me long before one of your white-faced race put foot upon the soil."

"And pray, who are you, if I may be so bold?" said Tom.

"Oh, I go by various names. I am the wild huntsman in some countries; the black miner in others. In this neighborhood I am known by the name of the black woodsman. I am he to whom the red men consecrated this spot, and in honor of whom they now and then roasted a white man, by way of sweet-smelling sacrifice. Since the red men have been exterminated by you white savages, I amuse myself by presiding at the persecutions of Quakers and Anabaptists; I am the great patron and prompter of slave-dealers, and the grand-master of the Salem witches."

"The upshot of all which is, that, if I mistake not," said Tom, sturdily, "you are he commonly called Old Scratch."

"The same, at your service!" replied the black man, with a half civil nod.

Such was the opening of this interview, according to the old story; though it has almost too familiar an air to be credited. One would think that to meet with such a singular personage, in this wild, lonely place, would have shaken any man's nerves; but Tom was a hard-minded fellow, not easily daunted, and he had lived so long with a ter-magant wife, that he did not even fear the devil.

It is said that after this commencement they had a long and earnest conversation together, as Tom returned homeward. The black man told him of great sums of money buried by Kidd the pirate, under the oak-trees on the high ridge, not far from the morass. All these were under his command, and protected by his power, so that none could find them but such as propitiated his favor. These he offered to place within Tom Walker's reach, having conceived an especial kindness for him; but they were to be had only on certain conditions. What these conditions were may be easily surmised, though Tom never disclosed them publicly. They must have been very hard, for he required time to think of them, and he was not a man to stick at trifles when money was in view. When they had reached the edge of the swamp, the stranger paused. "What proof have I that all you have been telling me is true?" said Tom. "There's my signature," said the black man, pressing his finger on Tom's forehead. So saying, he turned off among the thickest of the swamp, and seemed, as Tom said, to go down, down, down, into the earth, until nothing but his head and shoulders could be seen, and so on, until he totally disappeared.

When Tom reached home, he found the black print of a finger burnt, as it were, into his forehead, which nothing could obliterate.

The first news his wife had to tell him was the sudden death of Absalom Crowninshield, the rich buccaneer. It was announced in the papers with the usual flourish, that "A great man had fallen in Israel."

Tom recollected the tree which his black friend had just hewn down, and which was ready for burning. "Let the freebooter roast," said Tom; "who cares!" He now felt convinced that all he had heard and seen was no illusion.

He was not prone to let his wife into his confidence; but as this was an uneasy secret, he willingly shared it with her. All her avarice was awakened at the mention of hidden gold, and she urged her husband to comply with the black man's terms, and secure what would make them wealthy for life. However Tom might have felt disposed to sell himself to the devil, he was determined not to do so to oblige his wife; so he flatly refused, out of the mere spirit of contradiction. Many and bitter were the quarrels they had on the subject; but the more she talked, the more resolute was Tom not to be damned to please her.

At length she determined to drive the bargain on her own account, and if she succeeded, to keep all the gain to herself. Being of the same fearless temper as her husband, she set off for the old Indian fort towards the close of a summer's day. She was many hours absent. When she came back, she was reserved and sullen in her replies. She spoke something of a black man, whom she met about twilight hewing at the root of a tall tree. He was sulky, however, and would not come to terms: she was to go again with a propitiatory offering, but what it was she forbore to say.

The next evening she set off again for the swamp, with her apron heavily laden. Tom waited and waited for her, but in vain; midnight came, but she did not make her appearance: morning, noon, night returned, but still she did not come. Tom now grew uneasy for her safety, especially as he found she had carried off in her apron the silver tea-pot and spoons, and every portable article of value. Another night elapsed, another morning came; but no wife. In a word, she was never heard of more.

What was her real fate nobody knows, in consequence of so many pretending to know. It is one of those facts which have become confounded by a variety of historians. Some asserted that she lost her way among the tangled mazes of the swamp, and sank into some pit or slough; others, more uncharitable, hinted that she had eloped with the household booty, and made off to some other province; while others surmised that the tempter had decoyed her into a dismal quagmire, on the top of which her hat was found lying. In confirmation of this, it was said a great black man, with an axe on his shoulder, was seen late that very evening coming out of the swamp, carrying a bundle tied in a check apron, with an air of surly triumph.

The most current and probable story, however, observes, that Tom Walker grew so anxious about the fate of his wife and his property, that he set out at length to seek them both at the Indian fort. During a long summer's afternoon he searched about the gloomy place, but no wife was to be seen. He called her name repeatedly, but she was nowhere to be heard. The bittern alone responded to his voice, as he flew screaming by; or the bull-frog croaked dolefully from a neighboring pool. At length, it is said, just in the brown hour of twilight, when the owls began to hoot, and the bats to flit about, his attention was attracted by the clamor of carrion crows hovering about a cypress-tree. He looked up, and beheld a bundle tied in a check apron, and hanging in the branches of the tree, with a great vulture perched hard by, as if keeping watch upon it. He leaped with joy; for he recognized his wife's apron, and supposed it to contain the household valuables.

"Let us get hold of the property," said he, consolingly to himself, "and we will endeavor to do without the woman."

As he scrambled up the tree, the vulture spread its wide wings, and sailed off screaming, into the deep shadows of the forest. Tom seized the checked apron, but, woful sight! found nothing but a heart and liver tied up in it!

Such, according to this most authentic old story, was all that was to be found of Tom's wife. She had probably attempted to deal with the black man as she had been accustomed to deal with her husband; but though a female scold is generally considered a match for the devil, yet in this instance she appears to have had the worst of it. She must have died game, however; for it is said Tom noticed many prints of cloven feet deeply stamped upon the tree, and found handfuls of hair, that looked as if they had been plucked from the coarse black shock of the woodman. Tom knew his wife's prowess by experience. He shrugged his shoulders, as he looked at the signs of a fierce clapper-clawing. "Egad," said he to himself, "Old Scratch must have had a tough time of it!"

Tom consoled himself for the loss of his property, with the loss of his wife, for he was a man of fortitude. He even felt something like gratitude towards the black woodman, who, he considered, had done him a kindness. He sought, therefore, to cultivate a further acquaintance with him, but for some time without success; the old black-legs played shy, for whatever people may think, he is not always to be had for calling for: he knows how to play his cards when pretty sure of his game.

At length, it is said, when delay had whetted Tom's eagerness to the quick, and prepared him to agree to anything rather than not gain the promised treasure, he met the black man one evening in his usual woodman's dress, with his axe on his shoulder, sauntering along the swamp, and humming a tune. He affected to receive Tom's advances with great indifference, made brief replies, and went on humming his tune.

By degrees, however, Tom brought him to

business, and they began to haggle about the terms on which the former was to have the pirate's treasure. There was one condition which need not be mentioned, being generally understood in all cases where the devil grants favors; but there were others about which, though of less importance, he was inflexibly obstinate. He insisted that the money found through his means should be employed in his service. He proposed, therefore, that Tom should employ it in the black traffic; that is to say, that he should fit out a slave-ship. This, however, Tom resolutely refused: he was bad enough in all conscience; but the devil himself could not tempt him to turn slave-trader.

Finding Tom so squeamish on this point, he did not insist upon it, but proposed, instead, that he should turn usurer; the devil being extremely anxious for the increase of usurers, looking upon them as his peculiar people.

To this no objections were made, for it was just to Tom's taste.

"You shall open a broker's shop in Boston next month," said the black man.

"I'll do it to-morrow, if you wish," said Tom Walker.

"You shall lend money at two per cent a month."

"Egad, I'll charge four!" replied Tom Walker.

"You shall extort bonds, foreclose mortgages, drive the merchants to bankruptcy" —

"I'll drive them to the d——l," cried Tom Walker.

"You are the usurer for my money!" said black-legs with delight. "When will you want the rhino?"

"This very night."

"Done!" said the devil.

"Done!" said Tom Walker. — So they shook hands and struck a bargain.

A few days' time saw Tom Walker seated behind his desk in a counting-house in Boston.

His reputation for a ready-moneyed man, who would lend money out for a good consideration, soon spread abroad. Everybody remembers the time of Governor Belcher, when money was particularly scarce. It was a time of paper credit. The country had been deluged with government bills, the famous Land Bank had been established; there had been a rage for speculating; the people had run mad with schemes for new settlements; for building cities in the wilderness; land-jobbers went about with maps of grants, and townships, and Eldorados, lying nobody knew where, but which everybody was ready to purchase. In a word, the great speculating fever which breaks out every now and then in the country, had raged to an alarming degree, and every body was dreaming of making sudden fortunes from nothing. As usual the fever had subsided; the dream had gone off, and the imaginary fortunes with it; the patients were left in doleful plight, and the whole country re-sounded with the consequent cry of "hard times."

At this propitious time of public distress did Tom Walker set up as usurer in Boston. His door was soon thronged by customers. The needy and adventurous; the gambling speculator; the dreaming land-jobber; the thriftless tradesman; the merchant with cracked credit; in short, every one driven to raise money by desperate means and desperate sacrifices, hurried to Tom Walker.

Thus Tom was the universal friend of the needy, and acted like a "friend in need"; that is to say, he always exacted good pay and good security. In proportion to the distress of the applicant was the hardness of his terms. He accumulated bonds and mort-gages; gradually squeezed his customers closer and closer: and sent them at length, dry as a sponge, from his door.

In this way he made money hand over hand; became a rich and mighty man, and exalted his cocked hat upon 'Change. He built himself, as usual, a vast house, out of ostentation; but left the greater part of it unfinished and unfurnished, out of parsimony. He even set up a carriage in the fulness of his vainglory, though he nearly starved the horses which drew it; and as the ungreased wheels groaned and screeched on the axletrees, you would have thought you heard the souls of the poor debtors he was squeezing.

As Tom waxed old, however, he grew thoughtful. Having secured the good things of this world, he began to feel anxious about those of the next. He thought with regret on the bargain he had made with his black friend, and set his wits to work to cheat him out of the conditions. He became, therefore, all of a sudden, a violent church-goer. He prayed loudly and strenuously, as if heaven were to be taken by force of lungs. Indeed, one might always tell when he had sinned most during the week, by the clamor of his Sunday devotion. The quiet Christians who had been modestly and steadfastly travelling Zionward, were struck with self-reproach at seeing themselves so suddenly outstripped in their career by this new-made convert. Tom was as rigid in religious as in money matters; he was a stern supervisor and censurer of his neighbors, and seemed to think every sin entered up to their account became a credit on his own side of the page. He even talked of the expediency of reviving the persecution of Quakers and Anabaptists. In a word, Tom's zeal became as notorious as his riches.

Still, in spite of all this strenuous attention to forms, Tom had a lurking dread that the devil, after all, would have his due. That he might not be taken unawares, therefore, it is said he always carried a small Bible in his coat-pocket. He had also a great folio Bible on his counting-house desk, and would frequently be found reading it when people called on business; on such occasions he would lay his green spectacles in the book, to mark the place, while he turned round to drive some usurious bargain.

Some say that Tom grew a little crackbrained in his old days, and that, fancying his end approaching, he had his horse new shod, saddled and bridled, and buried with his feet uppermost; because he supposed that at the last day the world would be turned upside-down; in which case he should find his horse standing ready for mounting, and he was determined at the worst to give his old friend a run for it. This, however, is probably a mere old wives' fable. If he really did take such a precaution, it was totally superfluous; at least so says the authentic old legend, which closes his story in the following manner:

One hot summer afternoon in the dog-days, just as a terrible black thunder gust was coming up, Tom sat in his counting-house, in his white cap and India silk morning-gown. He was on the point of fore-closing a mortgage, by which he would complete the ruin of an unlucky land-speculator for whom he had professed the greatest friendship. The poor land-jobber begged him to grant a few months' indulgence. Tom had grown testy and irritated, and refused another day.

"My family will be ruined and brought upon the parish," said the land-jobber. "Charity begins at home," replied Tom; "I must take care of myself in these hard times."

"You have made so much money out of me," said the speculator.

Tom lost his patience and his piety. "The devil take me," said he, "if I have made a far-thing!"

Just then there were three loud knocks at the street door. He stepped out to see who was there. A black man was holding a black horse, which neighed and stamped with impatience.

"Tom, you're come for," said the black fellow, gruffly. Tom shrank back, but too late. He had left his little Bible at the bottom of his coat-pocket, and his big Bible on the desk buried under the mortgage he was about to foreclose: never was sinner taken more unawares. The black man whisked him like a child into the saddle, gave the horse the lash, and away he galloped, with Tom on his back, in the midst of the thunder-storm. The clerks stuck their pens behind their ears, and stared after him from the windows. Away went Tom Walker, dashing down the streets; his white cap bobbing up and down; his morning-gown fluttering in the wind, and his steed striking fire out of the pavement at every bound. When the clerks turned to look for the black man, he had disappeared.

Tom Walker never returned to foreclose the mortgage. A countryman, who lived on the border of the swamp, reported that in the height of the thunder-gust he had heard a great clattering of hoofs and a howling along the road, and running to the window caught sight of a figure, such as I have described, on a horse that galloped like mad across the fields, over the hills, and down into the black hemlock swamp towards the old Indian fort; and that shortly after a thunder-bolt falling in that direction seemed to set the whole forest in a blaze.

The good people of Boston shook their heads and shrugged their shoulders, but had been so much accustomed to witches and goblins, and tricks of the devil, in all kinds of shapes, from the first settlement of the colony, that they were not so much horror-struck as might have been expected. Trustees were appointed to take charge of Tom's effects. There was nothing, however, to administer upon. On searching his coffers, all his bonds and mortgages were found reduced to cinders. In place of gold and silver, his iron chest was filled with chips and shavings; two skeletons lay in his stable instead of his half-starved horses, and the very next day his great house took fire and burnt to the ground.

Such was the end of Tom Walker and his ill-gotten wealth. Let all griping money-brokers lay this story to heart. The truth of it is not to be doubted. The very hole under the oak-trees whence he dug Kidd's money is to be seen to this day; and the neighboring swamp and old Indian fort are often haunted in stormy nights by a figure on horseback, in morning-gown and white cap, which is doubtless the troubled spirit of the usurer. In fact the story has resolved itself into a proverb, and is the origin of that popular saying, so prevalent throughout New England, of "The Devil and Tom Walker."

Such, as nearly as I can recollect, was the purport of the tale told by the Cape-Cod whaler. There were divers trivial particulars which I have omitted, and which whiled away the morning very pleasantly, until the time of tide favorable to fishing being passed, it was proposed to land, and refresh ourselves under the trees, till the noontide heat should have abated.

We accordingly landed on a delectable part of the island of Manhatta, in that shady and embowered tract formerly under the domain of the ancient family of the Hardenbrooks. It was a spot well known to me in the course of the aquatic expeditions of my boyhood. Not far from where we landed there was an old Dutch family vault, constructed in the side of a bank, which had been an object of great awe and fable among my schoolboy associates. We had peered into it during one of our coasting voyages, and been startled by the sight of mouldering coffins and musty bones within; but what had given it the most fearful interest in our eyes, was its being in some way connected with the pirate wreck which lay rotting among the rocks of Hell Gate. There were stories also of smuggling connected with it, particularly relating to a time when this retired spot was owned by a noted burgher, called Ready Money Provost; a man of whom it was whispered that he had many mysterious dealings with parts beyond the seas. All these things, however, had been jumbled together in our minds in that vague way in which such themes are mingled up in the tales of boyhood.

While I was pondering upon these matters, my companions had spread a repast, from the contents of our well-stored pannier, under a broad chestnut, on the greensward which swept down to the water's edge. Here we solaced ourselves on the cool grassy carpet during the warm sunny hours of mid-day. While lolling on the grass, indulging in that kind of musing reverie of which I am fond, I summoned up the dusky recollections of my boyhood respecting this place, and repeated them like the imperfectly remembered traces of a dream, for the amusement of my companions. When I had finished, a worthy old burgher, John Josse Vandermoere, the same who once related to me the adventures of Dolph Heyliger, broke silence, and observed, that he recollected a story of money-digging, which occurred in this very neighborhood, and might account for some of the traditions which I had heard in my boyhood. As we knew him to be one of the most authentic narrators in the province, we begged him to let us have the particulars, and accordingly, while we solaced ourselves with a clean long pipe of Blase Moore's best tobacco, the authentic John Josse Vandermoere related the following tale.

Legend of the Three Beautiful Princesses

In old times there reigned a Moorish king in Granada, whose name was Mohamed, to which his subjects added the appellation of El Hayzari, or "The Left-handed." Some say he was so called on account of his being really more expert with his sinister than his dexter hand; others, because he was prone to take everything by the wrong end, or, in other words, to mar wherever he meddled. Certain it is, either through misfortune or mismanagement, he was continually in trouble; thrice was he driven from his throne, and on one occasion barely escaped to Africa with his life, in the disguise of a fisherman.* Still he was as brave as he was

*The reader will recognize the sovereign connected with the fortunes of the Abencerrages. His story appears to be a little fictionized in the legend. — W.I.

blundering; and though left-handed, wielded his cimeter to such purpose, that he each time re-established himself upon his throne by dint of hard fighting. Instead, however, of learning wisdom from adversity, he hardened his neck, and stiffened his left arm in wilfulness. The evils of a public nature which he thus brought upon himself and his kingdom may be learned by those who will delve into the Arabian annals of Granada; the present legend deals but with his domestic policy.

As this Mohamed was one day riding forth with a train of his courtiers, by the foot of the mountain of Elvira, he met a band of horsemen returning from a foray into the land of the Christians. They were conducting a long string of mules laden with spoil, and many captives of both sexes, among whom the monarch was struck with the appearance of a beautiful damsel, richly attired, who sat weeping on a low palfrey, and heeded not the consoling words of a *duenna* who rode beside her.

The monarch was struck with her beauty, and, on inquiring of the captain of the troop, found that she was the daughter of the Alcalde of a frontier fortress, that had been surprised and sacked in the course of the foray. Mohamed claimed her as his royal share of the booty, and had her conveyed to his harem in the Alhambra. There everything was devised to soothe her melancholy; and the monarch, more and more enamored, sought to make her his queen. The Spanish maid at first repulsed his addresses; he was an infidel; he was the open foe of her country; what was worse, he was stricken in years!

The monarch, finding his assiduities of no avail, determined to enlist in his favor the *duenna,* who had been captured with the lady. She was an Andalusian by birth, whose Christian name is forgotten, being mentioned in Moorish legends by no other appellation than that of the discreet Kadiga; and discreet in truth she was, as her whole history makes evident. No sooner had the Moorish king held a little private conversation with her, than she saw at once the cogency of his reasoning, and undertook his cause with her young mistress.

"Go to, now!" cried she; "what is there in all this to weep and wail about? Is it not better to be mistress of this beautiful palace, with all its gardens and fountains, than to be shut up within your father's old frontier tower? As to this Mohamed being an infidel, what is that to the purpose? You marry him, not his religion; and if he is waxing a little old, the sooner will you be a widow, and mistress of yourself; at any rate, you are in his power, and must either be a queen or a slave. When in the hands of a robber, it is better to sell one's merchandise for a fair price, than to have it taken by main force."

The arguments of the discreet Kadiga prevailed. The Spanish lady dried her tears, and became the spouse of Mohamed the Left-handed; she even conformed, in appearance, to the faith of her royal husband; and her discreet *duenna* immediately became a zealous convert to the Moslem doctrines: it was then the latter received the Arabian name of Kadiga, and was permitted to remain in the confidential employ of her mistress.

In due process of time the Moorish king was made the proud and happy father of three lovely daughters, all born at a birth; he could have wished they had been sons, but consoled himself with the idea that three daughters at a birth were pretty well for a man somewhat stricken in years, and left-handed!

As usual with all Moslem monarchs, he summoned his astrologers on this happy event. They cast the nativities of the three princesses, and shook their heads. "Daughters, O king!" said they, "are always precarious property; but these will most need your watchfulness when they arrive at a marriageable age; at that time gather them under your wings, and trust them to no other guardianship."

Mohamed the Left-handed was acknowledged to be a wise king by his courtiers, and was certainly so considered by himself. The prediction of the astrologers caused him but little disquiet, trusting to his ingenuity to guard his daughters and outwit the Fates.

The threefold birth was the last matrimonial trophy of the monarch; his queen bore him no more children, and died within a few years, bequeathing her infant daughters to his love, and to the fidelity of the discreet Kadiga.

Many years had yet to elapse before the princesses would arrive at that period of danger — the marriageable age. "It is good, however, to be cautious in time," said the shrewd monarch; so he determined to have them reared in the royal castle of Salobreña. This was a sumptuous palace, incrusted, as it were, in a powerful Moorish fortress on the summit of a hill overlooking the Mediterranean Sea. It was a royal retreat, in which the Moslem monarchs shut up such of their relatives as might endanger their safety; allowing them all kinds of luxuries and amusements, in the midst of which they passed their lives in voluptuous indolence.

Here the princesses remained, immured from the world, but surrounded by enjoyment, and attended by female slaves who anticipated their wishes. They had delightful gardens for their recreation, filled with the rarest fruits and flowers, with aromatic groves and perfumed baths. On three sides the castle looked down upon a rich valley, enamelled with all kinds of culture, and bounded by the lofty Alpuxarra mountains; on the other side it overlooked the broad sunny sea.

In this delicious abode, in a propitious climate, and under a cloudless sky, the three princesses grew up into wondrous beauty; but though all reared alike, they gave early tokens of diversity of character. Their names were Zayda, Zorayda, and Zorahayda; and such was their order of seniority, for there had been precisely three minutes between their births.

Zayda, the eldest, was of an intrepid spirit, and took the lead of her sisters in everything, as she had done in entering into the world. She was curious and inquisitive, and fond of getting at the bottom of things.

Zorayda had a great feeling for beauty, which was the reason, no doubt, of her delighting to regard her own image in a mirror or a fountain, and of her fondness for flowers, and jewels, and other tasteful ornaments.

As to Zorahayda, the youngest, she was soft and timid, and extremely sensitive, with a vast deal of disposable tenderness, as was evident from her number of pet-flowers, and pet-birds, and pet-animals, all of which she cherished with the fondest care. Her amusements, too, were of a gentle nature, and mixed up with musing and reverie. She would sit for hours in a balcony, gazing on the sparkling stars of a summer's night, or on the sea when lit up by the moon; and at such times, the song of a fisherman, faintly heard from the beach, or the notes of a Moorish flute from some gliding bark, sufficed to elevate her feelings into ecstasy. The least uproar of the elements, however, filled her with dismay; and a clap of thunder was enough to throw her into a swoon.

Years rolled on smoothly and serenely; the discreet Kadiga, to whom the princesses were confided, was faithful to her trust, and attended them with unremitting care.

The castle of Salobreña, as has been said, was built upon a hill on the sea-coast. One of the exterior walls straggled down the profile of the hill, until it reached a jutting rock over-hanging the sea, with a narrow sandy beach at its foot, laved by the rippling billows. A small watch-tower on this rock had been fitted up as a pavilion, with latticed windows to admit the sea-breeze. Here the princesses used to pass the sultry hours of mid-day.

The curious Zayda was one day seated at a window of the pavilion, as her sisters, reclining on ottomans, were taking the siesta or noontide slumber. Her attention was attracted to a galley which came coasting along, with measured strokes of the oar. As it drew near, she observed that it was filled with armed men. The galley anchored at the foot of the tower. A number of Moorish soldiers landed on the narrow beach, conducting several Christian prisoners. The curious Zayda awakened her sisters, and all three peeped cautiously through the close *jalousies* of the lattice which screened them from sight. Among the prisoners were three Spanish cavaliers, richly dressed. They were in the flower of youth, and of noble presence; and the lofty manner in which they carried themselves, though loaded with chains and surrounded with enemies, bespoke the grandeur of their souls. The princesses gazed with intense and breathless interest. Cooped up as they had been in this castle among female attendants, seeing nothing of the male sex but black slaves, or the rude fishermen of the sea-coast, it is not to be wondered at that the appearance of three gallant cavaliers, in the pride of youth and manly beauty, should produce some commotion in their bosom.

"Did ever nobler being tread the earth than that cavalier in crimson?" cried Zayda, the eldest of the sisters. "See how proudly he bears himself, as though all around him were his slaves!"

"But notice that one in green!" exclaimed Zorayda. "What grace! what elegance! what spirit!"

The gentle Zorahayda said nothing, but she secretly gave preference to the cavalier in blue.

The princesses remained gazing until the prisoners were out of sight; then, heaving long-drawn sighs, they turned round, looked at each other for a moment, and sat down, musing and pensive, on their ottomans.

The discreet Kadiga found them in this situation. They related what they had seen; and even the withered heart of the *duenna* was warmed. "Poor youths!" exclaimed she, "I'll warrant their captivity makes many a fair and high-born lady's heart ache in their native land! Ah! my children, you have little idea of the life these cavaliers lead in their own country. Such prankling at tournaments! such devotion to the ladies! such courting and serenading!"

The curiosity of Zayda was fully aroused; she was insatiable in her inquiries, and drew from the *duenna* the most animated pictures of the scenes of her youthful days and native land. The beautiful Zorayda bridled up, and slyly regarded herself in a mirror, when the theme turned upon the charms of the Spanish ladies; while Zorahayda suppressed a struggling sigh at the mention of moonlight serenades.

Every day the curious Zayda renewed her inquiries, and every day the sage *duenna* repeated her stories, which were listened to with profound interest, though with frequent sighs, by her gentle auditors. The discreet old woman awoke at length to the mischief she might be doing. She had been accustomed to think of the princesses only as children; but they had imperceptibly ripened beneath her eye, and now bloomed before her three lovely damsels of the marriageable age. It is time, thought the *duenna,* to give notice to the king.

Mohamed the Left-handed was seated one morning on a divan in a cool hall of the

Alhambra, when a slave arrived from the fortress of Salobreña, with a message from the sage Kadiga, congratulating him on the anniversary of his daughters' birthday. The slave at the same time presented a delicate little basket, decorated with flowers, within which, on a couch of vine and fig-leaves, lay a peach, an apricot, and a nectarine, with their bloom and down and dewy sweetness upon them, and all in the early stage of tempting ripeness. The monarch was versed in the Oriental language of fruits and flowers, and rapidly divined the meaning of this emblematical offering.

"So," said he, "the critical period pointed out by the astrologers is arrived: my daughters are at a marriageable age. What is to be done? They are shut up from the eyes of men; they are under the eyes of the discreet Kadiga, — all very good; but still they are not under my own eye, as was prescribed by the astrologers. I must gather them under my wing, and trust to no other guardianship."

So saying, he ordered that a tower of the Alhambra should be prepared for their reception, and departed at the head of his guards for the fortress of Salobreña, to conduct them home in person.

About three years had elapsed since

Mohamed had beheld his daughters, and he could scarcely credit his eyes at the wonderful change which that small space of time had made in their appearance. During the interval, they had passed that wondrous boundary line in female life which separates the crude, unformed, and thoughtless girl from the blooming, blushing, meditative woman. It is like passing from the flat, bleak, uninteresting plains of La Mancha to the voluptuous valleys and swelling hills of Andalusia.

Zayda was tall and finely formed, with a lofty demeanor and a penetrating eye. She entered with a stately and decided step, and made a profound reverence to Mohamed, treating him more as her sovereign than her father. Zorayda was of the middle height, with an alluring look and swimming gait, and a sparkling beauty, heightened by the assistance of the toilette. She approached her father with a smile, kissed his hand, and saluted him with several stanzas from a popular Arabian poet, with which the monarch was delighted. Zorahayda was shy and timid, smaller than her sisters, and with a beauty of that tender, beseeching kind which looks for fondness and protection. She was little fitted to command, like her elder sister, or to dazzle, like the second, but was rather formed to creep to the bosom of manly affection, to nestle within it, and be content. She drew near to her father, with a timid and almost faltering step, and would have taken his hand to kiss; but on looking up into his face, and seeing it beaming with a paternal smile, the tenderness of her nature broke forth, and she threw herself upon his neck.

Mohamed the Left-handed surveyed his blooming daughters with mingled pride and perplexity, for while he exulted in their charms, he bethought himself of the prediction of the astrologers. "Three daughters! three daughters!" muttered he repeatedly to himself, "and all of a marriageable age! Here's tempting Hesperian fruit, that requires a dragon watch!"

He prepared for his return to Granada, by sending heralds before him, commanding every one to keep out of the road by which he was to pass, and that all doors and windows should be closed at the approach of the princesses. This done, he set forth, escorted by a troop of black horsemen of hideous aspect, and clad in shining armor.

The princesses rode beside the king, closely veiled, on beautiful white palfreys, with velvet caparisons, embroidered with gold, and sweeping the ground; the bits and stirrups were of gold, and the silken bridles adorned with pearls and precious stones. The palfreys were covered with little silver bells, which made the most musical tinkling as they ambled gently along. Woe to the unlucky wight, however, who lingered in the way when he heard the tinkling of these bells! — the guards were ordered to cut him down without mercy.

The cavalcade was drawing near to Granada, when it overtook, on the banks of the river Xenil, a small body of Moorish soldiers with a convoy of prisoners. It was too late for the soldiers to get out of the way, so they threw themselves on their faces on the earth, ordering their captives to do the like. Among the prisoners were the three identical cavaliers whom the princesses had seen from the pavilion. They either did not understand, or were too haughty to obey the order, and remained standing and gazing upon the cavalcade as it approached.

The ire of the monarch was kindled at this flagrant defiance of his orders. Drawing his cimeter, and pressing forward, he was about to deal a left-handed blow that might have been fatal to at least one of the gazers, when the princesses crowded round him, and implored mercy for the prisoners; even the timid Zorahayda forgot her shyness, and became eloquent in their behalf. Mohamed paused, with uplifted cimeter, when the captain of the guard threw himself at his feet. "Let not your highness," said he, "do a deed that may cause great scandal throughout the kingdom. These are three brave and noble Spanish knights, who have been taken in battle, fighting like lions; they are of high birth, and may bring great ransoms." "Enough!" said the king. "I will spare their lives, but punish their audacity — let them be taken to the Vermilion Towers, and put to hard labor."

Mohamed was making one of his usual left-handed blunders. In the tumult and agitation of this blustering scene, the veils of the three princesses had been thrown back, and the radiance of their beauty revealed; and in prolonging the parley, the king had given that beauty time to have its full effect. In those days people fell in love much more suddenly than at present, as all ancient stories make manifest. It is not a matter of wonder, therefore, that the hearts of the three cavaliers were completely captured; especially as gratitude was added to their admiration. It is a little singular, however, though no less certain, that each of them was enraptured with a several beauty. As to the princesses, they were more than ever struck with the noble demeanor of the captives, and cherished in their breasts all that they had heard of their valor and noble lineage.

The cavalcade resumed its march; the three princesses rode pensively along on their tinkling palfreys, now and then stealing a glance behind in search of the Christian captives, and the latter were conducted to their allotted prison in the Vermilion Towers.

The residence provided for the princesses was one of the most dainty that fancy could devise. It was in a tower somewhat apart from the main palace of the Alhambra, though connected with it by the wall which encircled the whole summit of the hill. On one side it looked into the interior of the fortress, and had, at its foot, a small garden filled with the rarest flowers. On the other side it overlooked a deep embowered ravine separating the grounds of the Alhambra from those of the Generalife. The interior of the tower was divided into small fairy apartments, beautifully ornamented in the light Arabian style, surrounding a lofty hall, the vaulted roof of which rose almost to the summit of the tower. The walls and ceilings of the hall were adorned with arabesque and fretwork, sparkling with gold and with brilliant pencilling. In the centre of the marble pavement was an alabaster fountain, set round with aromatic shrubs and flowers, and throwing up a jet of water that cooled the whole edifice and had a lulling sound. Round the hall were suspended cages of gold and silver wire, containing singing-birds of the finest plumage or sweetest note.

The princesses had been represented as always cheerful when in the castle of the Salobreña; the king had expected to see them enraptured with the Alhambra. To his surprise, however, they began to pine, and grow melancholy, and dissatisfied with everything around them. The flowers yielded them no fragrance, the song of the nightingale disturbed their night's rest, and they were out of all patience with the alabaster fountain, with its eternal drop-drop and splash-splash, from morning till night and from night till morning.

The king, who was somewhat of a testy, tyrannical disposition, took this at first in high dudgeon; but he reflected that his daughters had arrived at an age when the female mind expands and its desires augment. "They are no longer children," said he to himself, "they are women grown, and require suitable objects to interest them." He put in requisition, therefore, all the dressmakers, and the jewellers, and the artificers in gold and silver throughout the Zacatin of Granada, and the princesses were over-whelmed with robes of silk, and tissue, and brocade, and cashmere shawls, and neck-laces of pearls and diamonds, and rings, and bracelets, and anklets, and all manner of precious things.

All, however, was of no avail; the prin-cesses continued pale and languid in the midst of their finery, and looked like three blighted rose-buds, drooping from one stalk. The king was at his wits' end. He had in general a laudable confidence in his own judgment, and never took advice. "The whims and caprices of three marriageable damsels, however, are sufficient," said he, "to puzzle the shrewdest head." So for once in his life he called in the aid of counsel.

The person to whom he applied was the experienced *duenna.*

"Kadiga," said the king, "I know you to be one of the most discreet women in the whole world, as well as one of the most trustworthy; for these reasons I have always continued you about the persons of my daughters. Fathers cannot be too wary in whom they repose such confidence; I now wish you to find out the secret malady that is preying upon the princesses, and to devise some means of restoring them to health and cheerfulness."

Kadiga promised implicit obedience. In fact she knew more of the malady of the princesses than they themselves. Shutting herself up with them, however, she endeavored to insinuate herself into their confidence.

"My dear children, what is the reason you are so dismal and downcast in so beautiful a place, where you have everything that heart can wish?"

The princesses looked vacantly round the apartment, and sighed.

"What more, then, would you have? Shall I get you the wonderful parrot that talks all languages, and is the delight of Granada?"

"Odious!" exclaimed the princess Zayda. "A horrid, screaming bird, that chatters words without ideas: one must be without brains to tolerate such a pest."

"Shall I send for a monkey from the rock of Gibraltar, to divert you with his antics?"

"A monkey! faugh!" cried Zorayda; "the detestable mimic of man. I hate the nauseous animal."

"What say you to the famous black singer Casem, from the royal harem, in Morocco? They say he has a voice as fine as a woman's."

"I am terrified at the sight of these black slaves," said the delicate Zorahayda; "besides I have lost all relish for music."

"Ah! my child, you would not say so," replied the old woman, slyly, "had you heard the music I heard last evening, from the three Spanish cavaliers whom we met on our journey. But bless me, children! what is the matter that you blush so and are in such a flutter?"

"Nothing, nothing, good mother; pray proceed."

"Well; as I was passing by the Vermilion Towers last evening, I saw the three cavaliers resting after their day's labor. One was playing on the guitar, so gracefully, and the others sang by turns; and they did it in such style, that the very guards seemed like statues, or men enchanted. Allah forgive me! I could not help being moved at hearing the songs of my native country. And then to see three such noble and handsome youths in chains and slavery!"

Here the kind-hearted old woman could not restrain her tears.

"Perhaps, mother, you could manage to procure us a sight of these cavaliers," said Zayda.

"I think," said Zorayda, "a little music would be quite reviving."

The timid Zorahayda said nothing, but threw her arms round the neck of Kadiga.

"Mercy on me!" exclaimed the discreet old woman, "what are you talking of, my children? Your father would be the death of us all if he heard of such a thing. To be sure, these cavaliers are evidently well-bred and high-minded youths; but what of that? they are the enemies of our faith, and you must not even think of them but with abhorrence."

There is an admirable intrepidity in the female will, particularly when about the marriageable age, which is not to be deterred by dangers and prohibitions. The princesses hung round their old *duenna,* and coaxed, and entreated, and declared that a refusal would break their hearts.

What could she do? She was certainly the most discreet old woman in the whole world, and one of the most faithful servants to the king; but was she to see three beautiful princesses break their hearts for the mere tinkling of a guitar? Besides, though she had been so long among the Moors, and changed her faith in imitation of her mistress, like a trusty follower, yet she was a Spaniard born, and had the lingerings of Christianity in her heart. So she set about to contrive how the wish of the princesses might be gratified.

The Christian captives, confined in the Vermilion Towers, were under the charge of a big-whiskered, broad-shouldered *renegado,* called Hussein Baba, who was reputed to have a most itching palm. She went to him privately, and slipping a broad piece of gold into his hand, "Hussein Baba," said she, "my mistresses the three princesses, who are shut up in the tower, and in sad want of amusement, have heard of the musical talents of the three Spanish cavaliers, and are desirous of hearing a specimen of their skill. I am sure you are too kind-hearted to refuse them so innocent a gratification."

"What! and to have my head set grinning over the gate of my own tower! for that would be the reward, if the king should discover it."

"No danger of anything of the kind; the affair may be managed so that the whim of the princesses may be gratified, and their father be never the wiser. You know the deep ravine outside of the walls which passes immediately below the tower. Put the three Christians to work there, and at the intervals of their labor, let them play and sing, as if for their own recreation. In this way the princesses will be able to hear them from the windows of the tower, and you may be sure of their paying well for your compliance."

As the good old woman concluded her harangue, she kindly pressed the rough hand of the *renegado,* and left within it another piece of gold.

Her eloquence was irresistible. The very next day the three cavaliers were put to work in the ravine. During the noontide heat, when their fellow-laborers were sleeping in the shade, and the guard nodding drowsily at his post, they seated themselves among the herbage at the foot of the tower, and sang a Spanish roundelay to the accompaniment of the guitar.

The glen was deep, the tower was high, but their voices rose distinctly in the stillness of the summer noon. The princesses listened from their balcony; they had been taught the Spanish language by their *duenna,* and were moved by the tenderness of the song. The discreet Kadiga, on the contrary, was terribly shocked. "Allah preserve us!" cried she, "they are singing a love-ditty, addressed to yourselves. Did ever mortal hear of such audacity? I will run to the slave-master and have them soundly bastinadoed."

"What! bastinado such gallant cavaliers, and for singing so charmingly!" The three beautiful princesses were filled with horror at the idea. With all her virtuous indignation, the good old woman was of a placable nature, and easily appeased. Besides, the music seemed to have a beneficial effect upon her young mistresses. A rosy bloom had already come to their cheeks, and their eyes began to sparkle. She made no further objection, therefore, to the amorous ditty of the cavaliers.

When it was finished, the princesses remained silent for a time; at length Zorayda took up a lute, and with a sweet, though faint and trembling voice, warbled a little Arabian air, the burden of which was, "The rose is concealed among her leaves, but she listens with delight to the song of the nightingale."

From this time forward the cavaliers worked almost daily in the ravine. The considerate Hussein Baba became more and more indulgent, and daily more prone to sleep at his post. For some time a vague intercourse was kept up by popular songs and romances, which in some measure responded to each other, and breathed the feelings of the parties. By degrees the princesses showed themselves at the balcony, when they could do so without being perceived by the guards. They conversed with the cavaliers also, by means of flowers, with the symbolical language of which they were mutually acquainted; the difficulties of their intercourse added to its charms, and strengthened the passion they had so singularly conceived; for love delights to struggle with difficulties, and thrives the most hardily on the scantiest soil.

The change effected in the looks and spirits of the princesses by this secret intercourse, surprised and gratified the left-handed king; but no one was more elated than the discreet Kadiga, who considered it all owing to her able management.

At length there was an interruption in this telegraphic correspondence; for several days the cavaliers ceased to make their appearance in the glen. The princesses looked out from the tower in vain. In vain they stretched their swan-like necks from the balcony; in vain they sang like captive nightingales in their cage: nothing was to be seen of their Christian lovers; not a note responded from the groves. The discreet Kadiga sallied forth in quest of intelligence, and soon returned with a face full of trouble. "Ah, my children!" cried she, "I saw what all this would come to, but you would have your way; you may now hang up your lutes on the willows. The Spanish cavaliers are ransomed by their families; they are down in Granada, and preparing to return to their native country."

The three beautiful princesses were in despair at the tidings. Zayda was indignant at the slight put upon them, in thus being deserted without a parting word. Zorayda wrung her hands and cried, and looked in the glass, and wiped away her tears, and cried afresh. The gentle Zorahayda leaned over the balcony and wept in silence, and her tears fell drop by drop among the flowers of the bank, where the faithless cavaliers had so often been seated.

The discreet Kadiga did all in her power to soothe their sorrow. "Take comfort, my children," said she, "this is nothing when you are used to it. This is the way of the world. Ah! when you are as old as I am, you will know how to value these men. I'll warrant these cavaliers have their loves among the Spanish beauties of Cordova and Seville, and will soon be serenading under their balconies, and thinking no more of the Moorish beauties in the Alhambra. Take comfort, therefore, my children, and drive them from your hearts."

The comforting words of the discreet Kadiga only redoubled the distress of the three princesses, and for two days they continued inconsolable. On the morning of the third the good old woman entered their apartment, all ruffling with indignation.

"Who would have believed such insolence in mortal man!" exclaimed she, as soon as she could find words to express herself; "but I am rightly served for having connived at this deception of your worthy father. Never talk more to me of your Spanish cavaliers."

"Why, what has happened, good Kadiga?" exclaimed the princesses in breathless anxiety.

"What has happened? — treason has happened! or, what is almost as bad, treason has been proposed; and to me, the most faithful of subjects, the trustiest of *duennas!* Yes, my children, the Spanish cavaliers have dared to tamper with me, that I should persuade you to fly with them to Cordova, and become their wives!"

Here the excellent old woman covered her face with her hands, and gave way to a violent burst of grief and indignation. The three beautiful princesses turned pale and red, pale and red, and trembled, and looked down, and cast shy looks at each other, but said nothing. Meantime the old woman sat rocking backward and forward in violent agitation, and now and then breaking out into exclamations: "That ever I should live to be so insulted! — I, the most faithful of servants!"

At length the eldest princess, who had

most spirit and always took the lead, approached her, and laying her hand upon her shoulder, "Well, mother," said she, "supposing we were willing to fly with these Christian cavaliers — is such a thing possible?"

The good old woman paused suddenly in her grief, looking up, "Possible," echoed she; "to be sure it is possible. Have not the cavaliers already bribed Hussein Baba, the *renegado* captain of the guard, and arranged the whole plan? But then, to think of deceiving your father! your father, who has placed such confidence in me!" Here the worthy woman gave way to a fresh burst of grief, and began again to rock backward and forward, and to wring her hands.

"But our father has never placed any confidence in us," said the eldest princess, "but has trusted to bolts and bars, and treated us as captives."

"Why, that is true enough," replied the old woman, again pausing in her grief; "he has indeed treated you most unreasonably, keeping you shut up here, to waste your bloom in a moping old tower, like roses left to wither in a flower-jar. But, then, to fly from your native land!"

"And is not the land we fly to the native land of our mother, where we shall live in freedom? And shall we not each have a youthful husband in exchange for a severe old father?"

"Why, that again is all very true; and your father, I must confess, is rather tyrannical; but what then," relapsing into her grief, "would you leave me behind to bear the brunt of his vengeance?"

"By no means, my good Kadiga; cannot you fly with us?"

"Very true, my child; and to tell the truth, when I talked the matter over with Hussein Baba, he promised to take care of me, if I would accompany you in your flight; but then, bethink you, my children, are you willing to renounce the faith of your father?"

"The Christian faith was the original faith of our mother," said the eldest princess; "I am ready to embrace it, and so, I am sure, are my sisters."

"Right again," exclaimed the old woman, brightening up; "it was the original faith of your mother, and bitterly did she lament on her deathbed that she had renounced it. I promised her then to take care of your souls, and I rejoice to see that they are now in a fair way to be saved. Yes, my children, I too was born a Christian, and have remained a Christian in my heart, and am resolved to return to the faith. I have talked on the subject with Hussein Baba, who is a Spaniard by birth, and comes from a place not far from my native town. He is equally anxious to see his own country, and to be reconciled to the Church; and the cavaliers have promised that, if we are disposed to become man and wife, on returning to our native land, they will provide for us handsomely."

In a word, it appeared that this extremely discreet and provident old woman had consulted with the cavaliers and the *renegado,* and had concerted the whole plan of escape. The eldest princess immediately assented to it, and her example, as usual, determined the conduct of her sisters. It is true, the youngest hesitated, for she was gentle and timid of soul, and there was a struggle in her bosom between filial feeling and youthful passion; the latter, however, as usual, gained the victory, and with silent tears and stifled sighs she prepared herself for flight.

The rugged hill on which the Alhambra is built was, in old times, perforated with subterranean passages cut through the rock and leading from the fortress to various parts of the city and to distant sally-ports on the banks of the Darro and the Xenil. They had been constructed at different times by the Moorish kings as means of escape from sudden insurrections, or of secretly issuing forth on private enterprises. Many of them are now entirely lost, while others remain, partly choked with rubbish, and partly walled up, — monuments of the jealous precautions and warlike stratagems of the Moorish government. By one of these passages Hussein Baba had undertaken to conduct the princesses to a sally-port beyond the walls of the city, where the cavaliers were to be ready with fleet steeds, to bear the whole party over the borders.

The appointed night arrived; the tower of the princesses had been locked up as usual, and the Alhambra was buried in deep sleep. Towards midnight the discreet Kadiga listened from the balcony of a window that looked into the garden. Hussein Baba, the *renegado,* was already below, and gave the appointed signal. The *duenna* fastened the end of a ladder of ropes to the balcony, lowered it into the garden and descended. The two eldest princesses followed her with beating hearts; but when it came to the turn of the youngest princess, Zorahayda, she hesitated and trembled. Several times she ventured a delicate little foot upon the ladder, and as often drew it back, while her poor little heart fluttered more and more the longer she delayed. She cast a wistful look back into the silken chamber; she had lived in it, to be sure, like a bird in a cage; but within it she was secure; who could tell what dangers might beset her should she flutter forth into the wide world! Now she bethought her of her gallant Christian lover, and her little foot was instantly upon the ladder; and anon she thought of her father, and shrank back. But fruitless is the attempt to describe the conflict in the bosom of one so young and tender and loving, but so timid and so ignorant of the world.

In vain her sisters implored, the *duenna* scolded, and the *renegado* blasphemed beneath the balcony: the gentle little Moorish maid stood doubting and wavering on the verge of elopement; tempted by the sweetness of the sin, but terrified at its perils.

Every moment increased the danger of discovery. A distant tramp was heard. "The patrols are walking their rounds," cried the *renegado;* "if we linger, we perish. Princess, descend instantly, or we leave you."

Zorahayda was for a moment in fearful agitation; then loosening the ladder of ropes, with desperate resolution she flung it from the balcony.

"It is decided!" cried she; "flight is now out of my power! Allah guide and bless ye, my dear sisters!"

The two eldest princesses were shocked at the thoughts of leaving her behind, and would fain have lingered, but the patrol was advancing; the *renegado* was furious, and they were hurried away to the subterraneous passage. They groped their way through a fearful labyrinth, cut through the heart of the mountain, and succeeded in reaching, undiscovered, an iron gate that opened outside of the walls. The Spanish cavaliers were waiting to receive them, disguised as Moorish soldiers of the guard, commanded by the *renegado.*

The lover of Zorahayda was frantic when he learned that she had refused to leave the tower; but there was no time to waste in lamentations. The two princesses were placed behind their lovers, the discreet Kadiga mounted behind the *renegado,* and they all set off at a round pace in the direction of the Pass of Lope, which leads through the mountains towards Cordova.

They had not proceeded far when they heard the noise of drums and trumpets from the battlements of the Alhambra.

"Our flight is discovered!" said the *renegado.*

"We have fleet steeds, the night is dark, and we may distance all pursuit," replied the cavaliers.

They put spurs to their horses, and scoured across the Vega. They attained the foot of the mountain of Elvira, which stretches like a promontory into the plain. The *renegado* paused and listened. "As yet," said he, "there is no one on our traces, we shall make good our escape to the mountains." While he spoke, a light blaze sprang up on the top of the watch-tower of the Alhambra.

"Confusion!" cried the *renegado,* "that bale fire will put all the guards of the passes on the alert. Away! away! Spur like mad, — there is no time to be lost."

Away they dashed — the clattering of their horses' hoofs echoed from rock to rock, as they swept along the road that skirts the rocky mountain of Elvira. As they galloped on, the bale fire of the Alhambra was answered in every direction; light after light blazed on the *atalayas,* or watch-towers of the mountains.

"Forward! forward!" cried the *renegado,* with many an oath, "to the bridge, — to the bridge, before the alarm has reached there!"

They doubled the promontory of the mountains, and arrived in sight of the famous Bridge of Pinos, that crosses a rushing stream often dyed with Christian and Moslem blood. To their confusion, the tower on the bridge blazed with lights and glittered with armed men. The *renegado* pulled up his steed, rose in his stirrups, and looked about him for a moment; then beckoning to the cavaliers, he struck off from the road, skirted the river for some distance, and dashed into its waters. The cavaliers called upon the princesses to cling to them, and did the same. They were borne for some distance down the rapid current, the surges roared round them, but the beautiful princesses clung to their Christian knights, and never uttered a complaint. The cavaliers attained the opposite bank in safety, and were conducted by the *renegado,* by rude and unfrequented paths and wild *barrancos,* through the heart of the mountains, so as to avoid all the regular passes. In a word, they succeeded in reaching the ancient city of Cordova; where their restoration to their country and friends was celebrated with great rejoicings, for they were of the noblest families. The beautiful princesses were forthwith received into the bosom of the Church, and, after being in all due form made regular Christians, were rendered happy wives.

In our hurry to make good the escape of the princesses across the river, and up the mountains, we forgot to mention the fate of the discreet Kadiga. She had clung like a cat to Hussein Baba in the scamper across the Vega, screaming at every bound, and drawing many an oath from the whiskered *renegado;* but when he prepared to plunge his steed into the river, her terror knew no bounds. "Grasp me not so tightly," cried Hussein Baba; "hold on by my belt and fear nothing." She held firmly with both hands by the leathern belt that girded the broad-backed *renegado;* but when he halted with the cavaliers to take breath on the mountain summit, the *duenna* was no longer to be seen.

"What has become of Kadiga?" cried the princesses in alarm.

"Allah alone knows!" replied the *renegado;* "my belt came loose when in the midst of the river, and Kadiga was swept with it down the stream. The will of Allah be done! but it was an embroidered belt, and of great price."

There was no time to waste in idle regrets; yet bitterly did the princesses bewail the loss of their discreet counsellor. That excellent old woman, however, did not lose more than half of her nine lives in the water; a fisherman, who was drawing his nets some distance down the stream, brought her to land, and was not a little astonished at his miraculous draught. What further became of the discreet Kadiga, the legend does not mention; certain it is that she evinced her discretion in never venturing within the reach of Mohamed the Left-handed.

Almost as little is known of the conduct of that sagacious monarch when he discovered the escape of his daughters, and the deceit practised upon him by the most faithful of servants. It was the only instance in which he had called in the aid of counsel, and he was never afterwards known to be guilty of a similar weakness. He took good care, however, to guard his remaining daughter, who had no disposition to elope; it is thought, indeed, that she secretly repented having remained behind: now and then she was seen leaning on the battlements of the tower, and looking mournfully towards the mountains in the direction of Cordova, and sometimes the notes of her lute were heard accompanying plaintive ditties, in which she was said to lament the loss of her sisters and her lover, and to bewail her solitary life. She died young, and, according to popular rumor, was buried in a vault beneath the tower, and her untimely fate has given rise to more than one traditionary fable.

The following legend, which seems in some measure to spring out of the foregoing story, is too closely connected with high historic names to be entirely doubted. The Count's daughter, and some of her young companions, to whom it was read in one of the evening *tertullias,* thought certain parts of it had much appearance of reality; and Dolores, who was much more versed than they in the improbable truths of the Alhambra, believed every word of it.

Legend of the Rose
of the Alhambra

For some time after the surrender of
Granada by the Moors, that delightful city
was a frequent and favorite residence of the
Spanish sovereigns, until they were frightened away by successive shocks of earthquakes, which toppled down various
houses, and made the old Moslem towers
rock to their foundation.

Many, many years then rolled away,
during which Granada was rarely honored
by a royal guest. The palaces of the nobility
remained silent and shut up; and the
Alhambra, like a slighted beauty, sat in
mournful desolation among her neglected
gardens. The Tower of the Infantas, once
the residence of the three beautiful Moorish
princesses, partook of the general desolation; the spider spun her web athwart the
gilded vault, and bats and owls nestled in

those chambers that had been graced by the presence of Zayda, Zorayda, and Zorahayda. The neglect of this tower may have been partly owing to some superstitious notions of the neighbors. It was rumored that the spirit of the youthful Zorahayda, who had perished in that tower, was often seen by moonlight seated beside the fountain in the hall, or moaning about the battlements, and that the notes of her silver lute would be heard at midnight by wayfarers passing along the glen.

At length the city of Granada was once more welcomed by the royal presence. All the world knows that Philip V. was the first Bourbon that swayed the Spanish sceptre. All the world knows that he married, in second nuptials, Elizabetta or Isabella (for they are the same), the beautiful princess of Parma; and all the world knows that by this chain of contingencies a French prince and an Italian princess were seated together on the Spanish throne. For a visit of this illustrious pair, the Alhambra was repaired and fitted up with all possible expedition. The arrival of the court changed the whole aspect of the lately deserted palace. The clangor of drum and trumpet, the tramp of steed about the avenues and outer court, the glitter of arms and display of banners about barbican and battlement, recalled the ancient and war-like glories of the fortress. A softer spirit, however, reigned within the royal palace. There was the rustling of robes and the cautious tread and murmuring voice of reverential courtiers about the ante-chambers, a loitering of pages and maids of honor about the gardens, and the sound of music stealing from open casements.

Among those who attended in the train of the monarchs was a favorite page of the queen, named Ruyz de Alarcon. To say that he was a favorite page of the queen was at once to speak his eulogium, for every one in the suite of the stately Elizabetta was chosen for grace, and beauty, and accomplishments. He was just turned of eighteen, light and lithe of form, and graceful as a young Antinous. To the queen he was all deference and respect, yet he was at heart a roguish stripling, petted and spoiled by the ladies about the court, and experienced in the ways of women far beyond his years.

This loitering page was one morning rambling about the groves of the Generalife, which overlook the grounds of the Alhambra. He had taken with him for his amusement a favorite gerfalcon of the queen. In the course of his rambles, seeing a bird rising from a thicket, he un-hooded the hawk and let him fly. The falcon towered high in the air, made a swoop at his quarry, but missing it, soared away, regardless of the calls of the page. The latter followed the truant bird with his eye, in its capricious flight, until he saw it alight upon the battlements of a remote and lonely tower, in the outer wall of the Alhambra, built on the edge of a ravine that separated the royal fortress from the grounds of the Generalife. It was in fact the "Tower of the Princesses."

The page descended into the ravine and approached the tower, but it had no entrance from the glen, and its lofty height rendered any attempt to scale it fruitless. Seeking one of the gates of the fortress, therefore, he made a wide circuit to that side of the tower facing within the walls.

A small garden, enclosed by a trellis-work of reeds overhung with myrtle, lay before the tower. Opening a wicket, the page passed between beds of flowers and thickets of roses to the door. It was closed and bolted. A crevice in the door gave him a peep into the interior. There was a small Moorish hall with fretted walls, light marble columns, and an alabaster fountain surrounded with flowers. In the centre hung a gilt cage containing a singing-bird; beneath it, on a chair, lay a tortoise-shell cat among reels of silk and other articles of female labor, and a guitar decorated with ribbons leaned against the fountain.

Ruyz de Alarcon was struck with these traces of female taste and elegance in a lonely and, as he had supposed, deserted tower. They reminded him of the tales of enchanted halls current in the Alhambra; and the tortoise-shell cat might be some spell-bound princess.

He knocked gently at the door. A beautiful face peeped out from a little window above, but was instantly withdrawn. He waited, expecting that the door would be opened, but he waited in vain; no footstep was to be heard within — all was silent. Had his senses deceived him, or was this beautiful apparition the fairy of the tower? He knocked again, and more loudly. After a little while the beaming face once more peeped forth; it was that of a blooming damsel of fifteen.

The page immediately doffed his plumed bonnet, and entreated in the most courteous accents to be permitted to ascend the tower in pursuit of his falcon.

"I dare not open the door, Señor," replied the little damsel, blushing, my aunt has forbidden it."

"I do beseech you, fair maid — it is the favorite falcon of the queen. I dare not return to the palace without it."

"Are you then one of the cavaliers of the court?"

"I am, fair maid; but I shall lose the queen's favor and my place, if I lose this hawk."

"*Santa Maria!* It is against you cavaliers of the court my aunt has charged me especially to bar the door."

"Against wicked cavaliers doubtless, but I am none of these, but a simple, harmless page, who will be ruined and undone if you deny me this small request."

The heart of the little damsel was touched by the distress of the page. It was a thousand pities he should be ruined for the want of so trifling a boon. Surely too he could not be one of those dangerous beings whom her aunt had described as a species of cannibal, ever on the prowl to make prey of thoughtless damsels; he was gentle and modest, and stood so entreatingly with cap in hand, and looked so charming.

The sly page saw that the garrison began to waver, and redoubled his entreaties in such moving terms that it was not in the nature of mortal maiden to deny him; so the blushing little warden of the tower descended, and opened the door with a trembling hand, and if the page had been charmed by a mere glimpse of her countenance from the window, he was ravished by the full-length portrait now revealed to him.

Her Andalusian bodice and trim *basquiña* set off the round but delicate symmetry of her form, which was as yet scarce verging into womanhood. Her glossy hair was parted on her forehead with scrupulous exactness, and decorated with a fresh-plucked rose, according to the universal custom of the country. It is true her complexion was tinged by the ardor of a southern sun, but it served to give richness to the mantling bloom of her cheek, and to heighten the lustre of her melting eyes.

Ruyz de Alarcon beheld all this with a single glance, for it became him not to tarry; he merely murmured his acknowledgments, and then bounded lightly up the spiral staircase in quest of his falcon.

He soon returned with the truant bird upon his fist. The damsel, in the meantime, had seated herself by the fountain in the hall, and was winding silk; but in her agitation she let fall the reel upon the pavement. The page sprang and picked it up, then dropping gracefully on one knee, presented it to her; but, seizing the hand extended to receive it, imprinted on it a kiss more fervent and devout than he had ever imprinted on the fair hand of his sovereign.

"Ave Maria, Señor!" exclaimed the damsel, blushing still deeper with confusion and surprise, for never before had she received such a salutation.

The modest page made a thousand apologies, assuring her it was the way at court of expressing the most profound homage and respect.

Her anger, if anger she felt, was easily pacified, but her agitation and embarrassment continued, and she sat blushing deeper and deeper, with her eyes cast down upon her work, entangling the silk which she attempted to wind.

The cunning page saw the confusion in the opposite camp, and would fain have profited by it, but the fine speeches he would have uttered died upon his lips; his attempts at gallantry were awkward and ineffectual; and to his surprise, the adroit page, who had figured with such grace and effrontery among the most knowing and experienced ladies of the court, found himself awed and abased in the presence of a simple damsel of fifteen.

In fact, the artless maiden, in her own modesty and innocence, had guardians more effectual than the bolts and bars prescribed by her vigilant aunt. Still, where is the female bosom proof against the first whisperings of love? The little damsel, with all her artlessness, instinctively comprehended all that the faltering tongue of the page failed to express, and her heart was fluttered at beholding, for the first time, a lover at her feet — and such a lover!

The diffidence of the page, though genuine, was short-lived, and he was recovering his usual ease and confidence, when a shrill voice was heard at a distance.

"My aunt is returning from mass!" cried the damsel in affright; "I pray you, Señor, depart."

"Not until you grant me that rose from your hair as a remembrance."

She hastily untwisted the rose from her raven locks. "Take it," cried she, agitated and blushing, "but pray begone."

The page took the rose, and at the same time covered with kisses the fair hand that gave it. Then, placing the flower in his bonnet, and taking the falcon upon his fist, he bounded off through the garden, bearing away with him the heart of the gentle Jacinta.

When the vigilant aunt arrived at the tower, she remarked the agitation of her niece, and an air of confusion in the hall; but

176

a word of explanation sufficed. "A gerfalcon had pursued his prey into the hall."

"Mercy on us! to think of a falcon flying into the tower. Did ever one hear of so saucy a hawk? Why, the very bird in the cage is not safe!"

The vigilant Fredegonda was one of the most wary of ancient spinsters. She had a becoming terror and distrust of what she denominated "the opposite sex," which had gradually increased through a long life of celibacy. Not that the good lady had ever suffered from their wiles, nature having set up a safeguard in her face that forbade all trespass upon her premises; but ladies who have least cause to fear for themselves are most ready to keep a watch over their more tempting neighbors.

The niece was the orphan of an officer who had fallen in the wars. She had been educated in a convent, and had recently been transferred from her sacred asylum to the immediate guardianship of her aunt, under whose overshadowing care she vegetated in obscurity, like an opening rose blooming beneath a brier. Nor indeed is this comparison entirely accidental; for, to tell the truth, her fresh and dawning beauty had caught the public eye, even in her seclusion, and, with that poetical turn common to the people of

Andalusia, the peasantry of the neighborhood had given her the appellation of "the Rose of the Alhambra."

The wary aunt continued to keep a faithful watch over her tempting little niece as long as the court continued at Granada, and flattered herself that her vigilance had been successful. It is true the good lady was now and then discomposed by the tinkling of guitars and chanting of love-ditties from the moonlit groves beneath the tower; but she would exhort her niece to shut her ears against such idle minstrelsy, assuring her that it was one of the arts of the opposite sex, by which simple maids were often lured to their undoing. Alas! what chance with a simple maid has a dry lecture against a moonlight serenade?

At length King Philip cut short his sojourn at Granada, and suddenly departed with all his train. The vigilant Fredegonda watched the royal pageant as it issued forth from the Gate of Justice and descended the great avenue leading to the city. When the last banner disappeared from her sight, she returned exulting to her tower, for all her cares were over. To her surprise, a light Arabian steed pawed the ground at the wicket-gate of the garden; — to her horror she saw through the thickets of roses a youth in gayly embroidered dress, at the feet of her niece. At the sounds of her footsteps he gave a tender adieu, bounded lightly over the barrier of reeds and myrtles, sprang upon his horse, and was out of sight in an instant.

The tender Jacinta, in the agony of her grief, lost all thought of her aunt's displeasure. Throwing herself into her arms, she broke forth into sobs and tears.

"Ay de mi!" cried she; "he's gone! he's gone! and I shall never see him more!"

"Gone! — who is gone? — what youth is that I saw at your feet?"

"A queen's page, aunt, who came to bid me farewell."

"A queen's page, child!" echoed the vigilant Fredegonda, faintly, "and when did you become acquainted with the queen's page?"

"The morning that the gerfalcon came into the tower. It was the queen's gerfalcon, and he came in pursuit of it."

"Ah silly, silly girl! know that there are no gerfalcons half so dangerous as these young prankling pages, and it is precisely such simple birds as thee that they pounce upon."

The aunt was at first indignant at learning that in despite of her boasted vigilance, a tender intercourse had been carried on by the youthful lovers, almost beneath her eye;

179

but when she found that her simple-hearted niece, though thus exposed, without the protection of bolt or bar, to all the machinations of the opposite sex, had come forth unsinged from the fiery ordeal, she consoled herself with the persuasion that it was owing to the chaste and cautious maxims in which she had, as it were, steeped her to the very lips.

While the aunt laid this soothing unction to her pride, the niece treasured up the oft-repeated vows of fidelity of the page. But what is the love of restless, roving man? A vagrant stream that dallies for a time with each flower upon its bank, then passes on, and leaves them all in tears.

Days, weeks, months, elapsed, and nothing more was heard of the page. The pomegranate ripened, the vine yielded up its fruit, the autumnal rains descended in torrents from the mountains; the Sierra Nevada became covered with a snowy mantle, and wintry blasts howled through the halls of the Alhambra — still he came not. The winter passed away. Again the genial spring burst forth with song and blossom and balmy zephyr; the snows melted from the mountains, until none remained but on the lofty summit of Nevada, glistening through the sultry summer air. Still nothing was heard of the forgetful page.

In the meantime the poor little Jacinta grew pale and thoughtful. Her former occupations and amusements were abandoned, her silk lay entangled, her guitar unstrung, her flowers were neglected, the notes of her bird unheeded, and her eyes, once so bright, were dimmed with secret weeping. If any solitude could be devised to foster the passion of a love-lorn damsel it would be such a place as the Alhambra, where everything seems disposed to produce tender and romantic reveries. It is a very paradise for lovers; how hard then to be alone in such a paradise — and not merely alone, but forsaken!

"Alas, silly child!" would the staid and immaculate Fredegonda say, when she found her niece in one of her desponding moods — "did I not warn thee against the wiles and deceptions of these men? What couldst thou expect, too, from one of a haughty and aspiring family — thou an orphan, the descendant of a fallen and impoverished line? Be assured, if the youth were true, his father, who is one of the proudest nobles about the court, would prohibit his union with one so humble and portionless as thou. Pluck up thy resolution therefore, and drive these idle notions from thy mind."

The words of the immaculate Fredegonda

only served to increase the melancholy of her niece, but she sought to indulge it in private. At a late hour one midsummer night, after her aunt had retired to rest, she remained alone in the hall of the tower, seated beside the alabaster fountain. It was here that the faithless page had first knelt and kissed her hand; it was here that he had often vowed eternal fidelity. The poor little damsel's heart was overladen with sad and tender recollections, her tears began to flow, and slowly fell drop by drop into the fountain. By degrees the crystal water became agitated, and — bubble — bubble — bubble — boiled up and was tossed about, until a female figure, richly clad in Moorish robes, slowly rose to view.

Jacinta was so frightened that she fled from the hall and did not venture to return. The next morning she related what she had seen to her aunt, but the good lady treated it as a fantasy of her troubled mind, or supposed she had fallen asleep and dreamt beside the fountain. "Thou hast been thinking of the story of the three Moorish princesses that once inhabited this tower," continued she, "and it has entered into thy dreams."

"What story, aunt? I know nothing of it."

"Thou hast certainly heard of the three princesses, Zayda, Zorayda, and Zorahayda, who were confined in this tower by the king their father, and agreed to fly with three Christian cavaliers. The two first accomplished their escape, but the third failed in her resolution, and, it is said, died in this tower."

"I now recollect to have heard of it," said Jacinta, "and to have wept over the fate of the gentle Zorahayda."

"Thou mayest well weep over her fate," continued the aunt, "for the lover of Zorahayda was thy ancestor. He long bemoaned his Moorish love; but time cured him of his grief, and he married a Spanish lady, from whom thou art descended."

Jacinta ruminated over these words. "That which I have seen is no fantasy of the brain," said she to herself, "I am confident. If indeed it be the spirit of the gentle Zorahayda, which I have heard lingers about this tower, of what should I be afraid? I'll watch by the fountain tonight — perhaps the visit will be repeated."

Towards midnight, when everything was quiet, she again took her seat in the hall. As the bell in the distant watch-tower of the Alhambra struck the midnight hour, the fountain was again agitated; and bubble — bubble — bubble — it tossed about the waters until the Moorish female again rose to view. She was young and beautiful; her dress was rich with jewels, and in her hand she held a silver lute. Jacinta trembled and was faint, but was reassured by the soft and plaintive voice of the apparition, and the sweet expression of her pale, melancholy countenance.

"Daughter of mortality," said she, "what aileth thee? Why do thy tears trouble my fountain, and thy sighs and plaints disturb the quiet watches of the night?"

"I weep because of the faithlessness of man, and I bemoan my solitary and forsaken state."

"Take comfort; thy sorrows may yet have an end. Thou beholdest a Moorish princess, who, like thee, was unhappy in her love. A Christian knight, thy ancestor, won my heart, and would have borne me to his native land and to the bosom of his church. I was a convert in my heart, but I lacked courage equal to my faith, and lingered till too late. For this the evil genii are permitted to have power over me, and I remain enchanted in this tower until some pure Christian will deign to break the magic spell. Wilt thou undertake the task?"

"I will," replied the damsel, trembling.

"Come hither, then, and fear not; dip thy hand in the fountain, sprinkle the water over me, and baptize me after the manner of thy faith; so shall the enchantment be dispelled, and my troubled spirit have repose."

The damsel advanced with faltering steps, dipped her hand in the fountain, collected water in the palm, and sprinkled it over the pale face of the phantom.

The latter smiled with ineffable benignity. She dropped her silver lute at the feet of Jacinta, crossed her white arms upon her bosom, and melted from sight, so that it seemed merely as if a shower of dewdrops had fallen into the fountain.

Jacinta retired from the hall filled with awe and wonder. She scarcely closed her eyes that night; but when she awoke at daybreak out of a troubled slumber, the whole appeared to her like a distempered dream. On descending into the hall, however, the truth of the vision was established, for beside the fountain she beheld the silver lute glittering in the morning sunshine.

She hastened to her aunt, to relate all that had befallen her, and called her to behold the lute as a testimonial of the reality of her story. If the good lady had any lingering doubts, they were removed when Jacinta touched the instrument, for she drew forth such ravishing tones as to thaw even the frigid bosom of the immaculate

Fredegonda, that region of eternal winter, into a genial flow. Nothing but supernatural melody could have produced such an effect.

The extraordinary power of the lute became every day more and more apparent. The wayfarer passing by the tower was detained, and, as it were, spellbound in breathless ecstasy. The very birds gathered in the neighboring trees, and hushing their own strains, listened in charmed silence.

Rumor soon spread the news abroad. The inhabitants of Granada thronged to the Alhambra to catch a few notes of the transcendent music that floated about the Tower of Las Infantas.

The lovely little minstrel was at length drawn forth from her retreat. The rich and powerful of the land contended who should entertain and do honor to her; or rather, who should secure the charms of her lute to draw fashionable throngs to their saloons. Wherever she went her vigilant aunt kept a dragon watch at her elbow, awing the throngs of impassioned admirers who hung in raptures on her strains. The report of her wonderful powers spread from city to city. Malaga, Seville, Cordova, all became successively mad on the theme; nothing was talked of throughout Andalusia but the beautiful minstrel of the Alhambra. How could it be otherwise among a people so musical and gallant as the Andalusians, when the lute was magical in its powers, and the minstrel inspired by love!

While all Andalusia was thus music mad, a different mood prevailed at the court of Spain. Philip V., as is well known, was a miserable hypochondriac, and subject to all kinds of fancies. Sometimes he would keep to his bed for weeks together, groaning under imaginary complaints. At other times he would insist upon abdicating his throne, to the great annoyance of his royal spouse, who had a strong relish for the splendors of a court and the glories of a crown, and guided the sceptre of her imbecile lord with an expert and steady hand.

Nothing was found to be so efficacious in dispelling the royal megrims as the power of music; the queen took care, therefore, to have the best performers, both vocal and instrumental, at hand, and retained the famous Italian singer Farinelli about the court as a kind of royal physician.

At the moment we treat of, however, a freak had come over the mind of this sapient and illustrious Bourbon that surpassed all former vagaries. After a long spell of imaginary illness, which set all the strains of Farinelli and the consultations of a whole orchestra of court fiddlers at defiance, the monarch fairly, in idea, gave up the ghost, and considered himself absolutely dead.

This would have been harmless enough, and even convenient both to his queen and courtiers, had he been content to remain in the quietude befitting a dead man; but to their annoyance he insisted upon having the funeral ceremonies performed over him, and, to their inexpressible perplexity, began to grow impatient, and to revile bitterly at them for negligence and disrespect, in leaving him unburied. What was to be done? To disobey the king's positive commands was monstrous in the eyes of the obsequious courtiers of a punctilious court — but to obey him, and bury him alive, would be downright regicide!

In the midst of this fearful dilemma a rumor reached the court of the female minstrel who was turning the brains of all Andalusia. The queen despatched missions in all haste to summon her to St. Ildefonso, where the court at that time resided.

Within a few days, as the queen with her maids of honor was walking in those stately gardens, intended, with their avenues and terraces and fountains, to eclipse the glories of Versailles, the far-famed minstrel was conducted into her presence. The imperial

Elizabetta gazed with surprise at the youthful and unpretending appearance of the little being that had set the world madding. She was in her picturesque Andalusian dress, her silver lute in hand, and stood with modest and downcast eyes, but with a simplicity and freshness of beauty that still bespoke her "the Rose of the Alhambra."

As usual she was accompanied by the ever-vigilant Fredegonda, who gave the whole history of her parentage and descent to the inquiring queen. If the stately Elizabetta had been interested by the appearance of Jacinta, she was still more pleased when she learnt that she was of a meritorious though impoverished line, and that her father had bravely fallen in the service of the crown. "If thy powers equal thy renown," said she, "and thou canst cast forth this evil spirit that possesses thy sovereign, thy fortunes shall henceforth be my care, and honors and wealth attend thee."

Impatient to make trial of her skill, she led the way at once to the apartment of the moody monarch.

Jacinta followed with downcast eyes through files of guards and crowds of courtiers. They arrived at length at a great chamber hung with black. The windows were closed to exclude the light of day; a number of yellow wax tapers in silver sconces diffused a lugubrious light, and dimly revealed the figures of mutes in mourning dresses, and courtiers who glided about with noiseless step and woebegone visage. In the midst of a funeral bed or bier, his hands folded on his breast, and the tip of his nose just visible, lay extended this would-be-buried monarch.

The queen entered the chamber in silence, and pointing to a footstool in an obscure corner, beckoned to Jacinta to sit down and commence.

At first she touched her lute with a faltering hand, but gathering confidence and animation as she proceeded, drew forth such soft aërial harmony, that all present could scarce believe it mortal. As to the monarch, who had already considered himself in the world of spirits, he set it down for some angelic melody or the music of the spheres. By degrees the theme was varied, and the voice of the minstrel accompanied the instrument. She poured forth one of the legendary ballads treating of the ancient glories of the Alhambra and the achievements of the Moors. Her whole soul entered into the theme, for with the recollections of the Alhambra was associated the story of her love. The funeral-chamber resounded with the animating strain. It entered into the gloomy heart of the monarch. He raised his head and gazed around: he sat up on his couch, his eye began to kindle — at length, leaping upon the floor, he called for sword and buckler.

The triumph of music, or rather of the enchanted lute, was complete; the demon of melancholy was cast forth; and, as it were, a dead man brought to life. The windows of the apartment were thrown open; the glorious effulgence of Spanish sunshine burst into the late lugubrious chamber; all eyes sought the lovely enchantress, but the lute had fallen from her hand, she had sunk upon the earth, and the next moment was clasped to the bosom of Ruyz de Alarcon.

The nuptials of the happy couple were celebrated soon afterwards with great splendor, and the Rose of the Alhambra became the ornament and delight of the court. "But hold — not so fast" — I hear the reader exclaim; "this is jumping to the end of a story at a furious rate! First let us know how Ruyz de Alarcon managed to account to Jacinta for his long neglect?" Nothing more easy; the venerable, time-honored excuse, the opposition to his wishes by a proud, pragmatical old father; besides, young people who really like one another soon come to an amicable understanding, and bury all past grievances when once they meet.

But how was the proud, pragmatical old father reconciled to the match?

Oh! as to that, his scruples were easily overcome by a word or two from the queen; especially as dignities and rewards were showered upon the blooming favorite of royalty. Besides, the lute of Jacinta, you know, possessed a magic power, and could control the most stubborn head and hardest breast.

And what came of the enchanted lute?

Oh, that is the most curious matter of all, and plainly proves the truth of the whole story. That lute remained for some time in the family, but was purloined and carried off, as was supposed, by the great singer Farinelli, in pure jealousy. At his death it passed into other hands in Italy, who were ignorant of its mystic powers, and melting down the silver, transferred the strings to an old Cremona fiddle. The strings still retain something of their magic virtues. A word in the reader's ear, but let it go no further: that fiddle is now bewitching the whole world, — it is the fiddle of Paganini!

From *The Alhambra*

The Creole Village

A Sketch From a Steamboat
[First published in 1837]

In travelling about our motley country, I am often reminded of Ariosto's account of the moon, in which the good paladin Astolpho found everything garnered up that had been lost on earth. So I am apt to imagine that many things lost in the Old World are treasured up in the New; having been handed down from generation to generation, since the early days of the colonies. A European antiquary, therefore, curious in his researches after the ancient and almost obliterated customs and usages of his country, would do well to put himself upon the track of some early band of emigrants, follow them across the Atlantic, and rummage among their descendants on our shores.

In the phraseology of New England might be found many an old English provincial phrase long since obsolete in the parent country, with some quaint relics of the Roundheads; while Virginia cherishes peculiarities characteristic of the days of Elizabeth and Sir Walter Raleigh.

In the same way, the sturdy yeomanry of New Jersey and Pennsylvania keep up many usages fading away in ancient Germany; while many an honest, broad bottomed custom, nearly extinct in venerable Holland, may be found flourishing in pristine vigor and luxuriance in Dutch villages, on the banks of the Mohawk and the Hudson.

In no part of our country, however, are the customs and peculiarities imported from the Old World by the earlier settlers kept up with more fidelity than in the little, poverty-stricken villages of Spanish and French origin, which border the rivers of ancient Louisiana. Their population is generally made up of the descendants of those nations, married and interwoven together, and occasionally crossed with a slight dash of the Indian. The French character, however, floats on top, as, from its buoyant qualities, it is sure to do, whenever it forms a particle, however small, of an intermixture.

In these serene and dilapidated villages, art and nature stand still, and the world forgets to turn round. The revolutions that distract other parts of this mutable planet, reach not here, or pass over without leaving any trace. The fortunate inhabitants have none of that public spirit which extends its cares beyond its horizon, and imports trouble and perplexity from all quarters in newspapers. In fact, newspapers are almost unknown in these villages; and, as French is the current language, the inhabitants have little community of opinion with their republican neighbors. They retain, therefore, their old habits of passive obedience to the decrees of government, as though they still lived under the absolute sway of colonial commandants, instead of being part and parcel of the sovereign people, and having a voice in public legislation.

A few aged men, who have grown gray on their hereditary acres, and are of the good old colonial stock, exert a patriarchal sway in all matters of public and private import; their opinions are considered oracular, and their word is law.

The inhabitants, moreover, have none of that eagerness for gain, and rage for improvement, which keep our people continually on the move, and our country towns incessantly in a state of transition. There the magic phrases, "town lots," "water privileges," "railroads," and other comprehensive and soul-stirring words from the speculator's vocabulary, are never heard. The residents dwell in the houses built by their forefathers, without thinking of enlarging or modernizing them, or pulling them down and turning them into granite stores. The trees under which they have been born, and have played in infancy, flourish undisturbed; though, by cutting them down, they might open new streets, and put money in their pockets. In a word, the almighty dollar, that great object of universal devotion throughout our land, seems to have no genuine devotees in these peculiar villages; and unless some of its missionaries penetrate there, and erect banking-houses and other pious shrines, there is no knowing how long the inhabitants may remain in their present state of contented poverty.

In descending one of our great western rivers in a steamboat, I met with two worthies from one of these villages, who had been on a distant excursion, the longest they had ever made, as they seldom ventured far from home. One was the great man, or Grand Seigneur of the village; not that he enjoyed any legal privileges or power there, everything of the kind having been done away when the province was ceded by France to the United States. His sway over his neighbors was merely one of custom and convention, out of deference to his family. Besides, he was worth full fifty thousand dollars, an amount almost equal, in the imaginations of the villagers, to the treasures of King Solomon.

This very substantial old gentleman, though of the fourth or fifth generation in this country, retained the true Gallic feature and deportment, and reminded me of one of those provincial potentates that are to be met with in the remote parts of France. He was of a large frame, a ginger-bread complexion, strong features, eyes that stood out like glass knobs, and a prominent nose, which he frequently regaled from a gold snuff-box, and occasionally blew with a colored handkerchief, until it sounded like a trumpet.

He was attended by an old negro, as black as ebony, with a huge mouth, in a continual grin; evidently a privileged and favorite servant, who had grown up and grown old with him. He was dressed in creole style, with white jacket and trousers, a stiff shirt-collar, that threatened to cut off his ears, a bright Madras handkerchief tied round his head, and large gold ear-rings. He was the politest negro I met with in a western tour, and that is saying a great deal, for, excepting the Indians, the negroes are the most gentleman-like personages to be met with in those parts. It is true they differ from the Indians in being a little extra polite and complimentary. He was also one of the merriest; and here, too, the negroes, however we may deplore their unhappy condition, have the advantage of their masters. The whites are, in general, too free and prosperous to be merry. The cares of maintaining their rights and liberties, adding to their wealth, and making presidents engross all their thoughts and dry up all the moisture of their souls. If you hear a broad, hearty, devil-may-care laugh, be assured it is a negro's.

Besides this African domestic, the seigneur of the village had another no less cherished and privileged attendant. This was a huge dog, of the mastiff breed, with a deep, hanging mouth, and a look of surly gravity. He walked about the cabin with the air of a dog perfectly at home, and who had paid for his passage. At dinner-time he took his seat beside his master, giving him a glance now and then out of a corner of his eye, which bespoke perfect confidence that he would not be forgotten. Nor was he. Every now and then a huge morsel would be thrown to him, peradventure the half-picked leg of a fowl, which he would receive with a snap like the springing of a steel trap, — one gulp, and all was down; and a glance of the eye told his master that he was ready for another consignment.

The other village worthy, travelling in company with the seigneur, was of a totally different stamp. Small, thin, and weazen-faced, as Frenchmen are apt to be represented in caricature, with a bright, squirrel-like eye, and a gold ring in his ear. His dress was flimsy, and sat loosely on his frame, and he had altogether the look of one with but little coin in his pocket. Yet, though one of the poorest, I was assured he was one of the merriest and most popular personages in his native village.

Compère Martin, as he was commonly called, was the factotum of the place — sportsman, schoolmaster, and land-surveyor. He could sing, dance, and above all, play on the fiddle, an invaluable accomplishment in an old French creole village, for the inhabitants have a hereditary love for balls and *fêtes*. If they work but little, they dance a great deal; and a fiddle is the joy of their heart.

What had sent Compère Martin travelling with the Grand Seigneur I could not learn. He evidently looked up to him with great deference, and was assiduous in rendering

him petty attentions; from which I concluded that he lived at home upon the
crumbs which fell from his table. He was
gayest when out of his sight, and had his
song and his joke when forward among the
deck passengers; but, altogether, Compère
Martin was out of his element on board of a
steamboat. He was quite another being, I
am told, when at home in his own village.

Like his opulent fellow-traveller, he too
had his canine follower and retainer, — and
one suited to his different fortunes, — one
of the civilest, most unoffending little dogs
in the world. Unlike the lordly mastiff, he
seemed to think he had no right on board of
the steamboat; if you did but look hard at
him, he would throw himself upon his back,
and lift up his legs, as if imploring mercy. At
table he took his seat a little distance from
his master; not with the bluff, confident air
of the mastiff, but quietly and diffidently;
his head on one side, with one car dubiously
slouched, the other hopefully cocked up; his
under-teeth projecting beyond his black
nose, and his eye wistfully following each
morsel that went into his master's mouth.

If Compère Martin now and then should
venture to abstract a morsel from his plate,
to give to his humble companion, it was edi-
fying to see with what diffidence the exem-

plary little animal would take hold of it, with the very tip of his teeth, as if he would almost rather not, or was fearful of taking too great a liberty. And then with what decorum would he eat it! How many efforts would he make in swallowing it, as if it stuck in his throat; with what daintiness would he lick his lips; and then with what an air of thankfulness would he resume his seat, with his teeth once more projecting beyond his nose, and an eye of humble expectation fixed upon his master.

It was late in the afternoon when the steamboat stopped at the village which was the residence of these worthies. It stood on the high bank of the river, and bore traces of having been a frontier trading-post. There were the remains of stockades that once protected it from the Indians, and the houses were in the ancient Spanish and French colonial taste, the place having been successively under the domination of both those nations prior to the cession of Louisiana to the United States.

The arrival of the seigneur of fifty thousand dollars, and his humble companion, Compère Martin, had evidently been looked forward to as an event in the village. Numbers of men, women, and children, white, yellow, and black, were collected on the river bank; most of them clad in old-fashioned French garments, and their heads decorated with colored handkerchiefs, or white nightcaps. The moment the steamboat came within sight and hearing, there was a waving of handkerchiefs, and a screaming and bawling of salutations and felicitations, that baffle all description.

The old gentleman of fifty thousand dollars was received by a train of relatives, and friends, and children, and grandchildren, whom he kissed on each cheek, and who formed a procession in his rear, with a legion of domestics, of all ages, following him to a large, old-fashioned French house, that domineered over the village.

His black *valet de chambre,* in white jacket and trousers, and gold ear-rings, was met on the shore by a boon, though rustic companion, a tall negro fellow, with a long good-humored face, and the profile of a horse, which stood out from beneath a narrow-rimmed straw hat, stuck on the back of his head. The explosions of laughter of these two varlets on meeting and exchanging compliments, were enough to electrify the country round.

The most hearty reception, however, was that given to Compère Martin. Everybody, young and old, hailed him before he got to land. Everybody had a joke for Compère Martin, and Compère Martin had a joke for everybody. Even his little dog appeared to partake of his popularity, and to be caressed by every hand. Indeed, he was quite a different animal the moment he touched the land. Here he was at home; here he was of consequence. He barked, he leaped, he frisked about his old friends, and then would skim round the place in a wide circle, as if mad.

I traced Compère Martin and his little dog to their home. It was an old ruinous Spanish house, of large dimensions, with verandas overshadowed by ancient elms. The house had probably been the residence, in old times, of the Spanish commandant. In one wing of this crazy, but aristocratical abode, was nestled the family of my fellow-traveller; for poor devils are apt to be magnificently clad and lodged, in the cast-off clothes and abandoned palaces of the great and wealthy.

The arrival of Compère Martin was welcomed by a legion of women, children, and mongrel curs; and, as poverty and gayety generally go hand-in-hand among the French and their descendants, the crazy mansion soon resounded with loud gossip and light-hearted laughter.

As the steamboat paused a short time at the village, I took occasion to stroll about the place. Most of the houses were in the French taste, with casements and rickety verandas, but most of them in flimsy and ruinous condition. All the wagons, ploughs, and other utensils about the place were of ancient and inconvenient Gallic construction, such as had been brought from France in the primitive days of the colony. The very looks of the people reminded me of the villages of France.

From one of the houses came the hum of a spinning-wheel, accompanied by a scrap of an old French *chanson,* which I have heard many a time among the peasantry of Languedoc, doubtless a traditional song, brought over by the first French emigrants, and handed down from generation to generation.

Half a dozen young lasses emerged from the adjacent dwellings, reminding me, by their light step and gay costume, of scenes in ancient France, where taste in dress comes natural to every class of females. The trim bodice and colored petticoat, and little apron, with its pockets to receive the hands when in an attitude for conversation; the colored kerchief wound tastefully round the head, with a coquettish knot perking above one ear; and the neat slipper and tight-drawn stocking, with its braid of narrow ribbon embracing the ankle where it peeps from its mysterious curtain. It is from this ambush that Cupid sends his most inciting arrows.

While I was musing upon the recollections thus accidentally summoned up, I heard the sound of a fiddle from the mansion of Compère Martin, the signal, no doubt, for a joyous gathering. I was disposed to turn my steps thither, and witness the festivities of one of the very few villages I had met with in my wide tour that was yet poor enough to be merry; but the bell of the steamboat summoned me to re-embark.

As we swept away from the shore, I cast back a wistful eye upon the moss-grown roofs and ancient elms of the village, and prayed that the inhabitants might long retain their happy ignorance, their absence of all enterprise and improvement, their respect for the fiddle, and their contempt for the almighty dollar.* I fear, however, my

---

*This phrase, used for the first time in this sketch, has since passed into current circulation, and by some has been questioned as savoring of irreverence. The author, therefore, owes it to his orthodoxy to declare that no irreverence was intended

prayer is doomed to be of no avail. In a little while the steamboat whirled me to an American town, just springing into bustling and prosperous existence.

The surrounding forest had been laid out in town lots; frames of wooden buildings were rising from among stumps and burnt trees. The place already boasted a courthouse, a jail, and two banks, all built of pine boards, on the model of Grecian temples. There were rival hotels, rival churches, and rival newspapers; together with the usual number of judges and generals and governors; not to speak of doctors by the dozen, and lawyers by the score.

The place, I was told, was in an astonishing career of improvement, with a canal and two railroads in embryo. Lots doubled in price every week; everybody was speculating in land; everybody was rich; and everybody was growing richer. The community, however, was torn to pieces by new doctrines in religion and in political economy; there were camp-meetings, and agrarian meetings; and an election was at hand, which, it was expected, would throw the whole country into a paroxysm.

---

even to the dollar itself; which he is aware is daily becoming more and more an object of worship. — W.I.

Alas! with such an enterprising neighbor, what is to become of the poor little creole village!

From *Wolfert's Roost*

About the Author

Washington Irving (1783–1859), born the year the United States won its independence, was the first American literary artist to earn his living solely through his writings and the first to enjoy international acclaim. In addition to his long public service as a diplomat, Irving was amazingly prolific: his collected works fill forty volumes that encompass essays, history, travel writings, and multivolume biographies of Columbus and Washington (Neider's abridged edition, *George Washington: A Biography*, is also available from Da Capo Press.) But it is Irving's mastery of suspense, characterization, tempo, and irony that transforms his fiction into virtuoso performances, earning him his reputation as the Father of the American Short Story.

Neider has gathered all 61 of Irving's tales, originally scattered throughout his many collections of nonfiction essays and sketches, into one magnificent volume. To-gether, they reveal his wide range: besides the expected classics like "Rip Van Winkle," "The Spectre Bridegroom," "The Legend of Sleepy Hollow," and "The Devil and Tom Walker," his fiction embraces realistic tales, ghost stories, parodies, legends, fables, and satires. For those familiar only with second-hand retellings of Irving's most famous tales, this collection offers the opportunity to step inside Washington Irving's imagina-tion and partake of its innumerable and timeless pleasures.

Charles Neider is a noted literary critic, editor, and novelist. His many books as ed-itor include Washington Irving's *George Washington: A Biography*, *The Complete Humorous Sketches and Tales of Mark Twain*, *The Great West: A Treasury of First-hand Accounts* (all three available from Da Capo Press), *The Complete Essays of Mark Twain*, *The Autobiography of Mark Twain*, and *The Complete Short Stories of Robert Louis Stevenson*. He lives in Princeton, New Jersey.

The employees of Thorndike Press hope you have enjoyed this Large Print book. All our Thorndike and Wheeler Large Print titles are designed for easy reading, and all our books are made to last. Other Thorndike Press Large Print books are available at your library, through selected bookstores, or directly from us.

For information about titles, please call:

(800) 223-1244

or visit our Web site at:

www.gale.com/thorndike
www.gale.com/wheeler

To share your comments, please write:

Publisher
Thorndike Press
295 Kennedy Memorial Drive
Waterville, ME 04901